# COMPREHENSION AND GRAMMAR

PASCAL PRESS

# CONTENTS

## Term 1

### Fiction Unit

Lexile Levels 440L–480L



### Nonfiction Unit

Lexile Levels 460L–520L



## Term 2

### Fiction Unit

Lexile Levels 480L–520L



### Nonfiction Unit

Lexile Levels 520L–560L

## Term 3

### Fiction Unit

Lexile Levels 520L–580L



### Nonfiction Unit

Lexile Levels 560L–600L



## Term 4

### Fiction Unit

Lexile Levels 600L–620L



### Nonfiction Unit

Lexile Levels 620L–640L

# INTRODUCTION

**Reading comprehension** is the ability to understand and interpret text. To become confident and competent readers, students need to learn how to understand the literal meaning of a text and its vocabulary, and also its implied and inferred meaning.

This workbook is organised into four terms of work with 40 step-by-step lessons that focus on specific comprehension skills. To further support students, 8 grammar lessons target language usage. By looking carefully at words, clauses and sentences, students are better equipped to understand the texts they read. Each terms ends with a summative assessment that identifies students' strengths and rewards progress.

## Step-by-step Comprehension

The 40 comprehension lessons teach key strategies for students to use when they read. Each lesson uses a levelled extract and focuses on a single comprehension strategy, with clear, easy-to-read instructions.

Students find key details in the text and highlight words and phrases. This ensures students have knowledge of the text before answering comprehension questions. The extracts are organised in a progressive sequence with clear modelling and built-in support. By focusing on a single strategy at a time, students develop their literal, inferential and critical comprehension skills, as well as extending their vocabulary.

## Integrated Grammar

The eight grammar lessons in this book aim to help students understand how the English language system works, and how to apply this knowledge to texts.

Each lesson teaches a key concept in grammar. The focus is on connecting grammatical terms to text in meaningful ways. The instructional information box explains the concept and shows examples. Students then annotate a text and answer questions to identify the grammar in action. Questions increase in difficulty and include NAPLAN-style questions. The grammar lessons help students comprehend and connect with a broad range of texts.

## The Reading Eggspress Online Lessons

Reading Eggspress provides a comprehensive and systematic online program that models, scaffolds and supports reading comprehension. The 220 lessons have been organised in a clear progression to develop reading comprehension skills for students in Years 1–6. Each lesson includes built-in motivational elements to reward efforts and boost students' enthusiasm for reading.

The workbook lessons can be completed as a stand-alone reading comprehension course, but when combined with the online lessons they act as a powerful boost to students' reading comprehension skills. Students using the online program show significant year-on-year improvements in both reading comprehension skills and higher reading levels, as highlighted in the program's detailed reporting module.

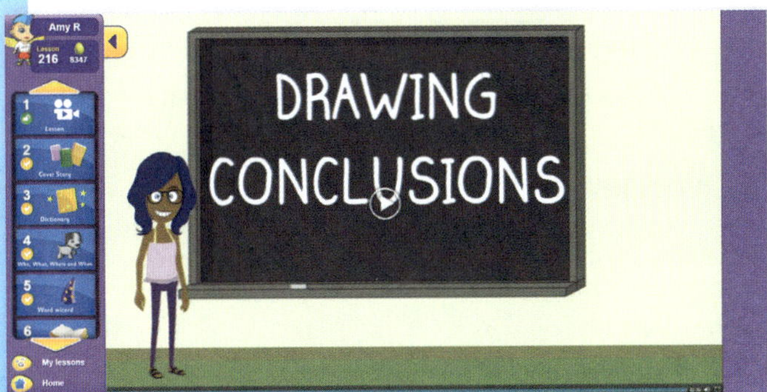

Engaging lessons

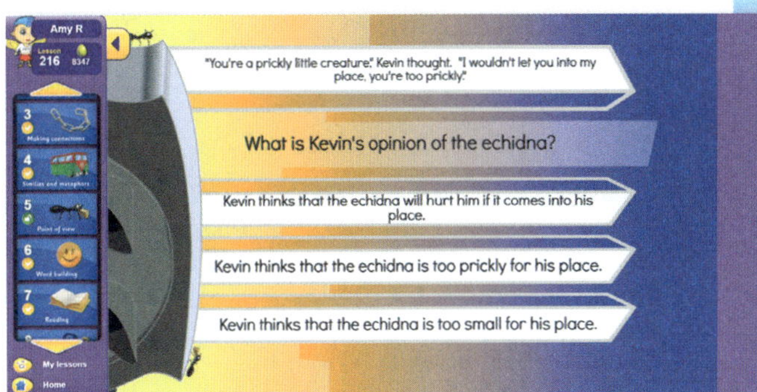

Interactive activities

## The Library 2500+ ebooks

Students can practise their comprehension skills by reading ebooks in the Reading Eggspress Library. Search by topic, series, author, Lexile, reading age or book title to find the perfect book. With illustrated chapter books, full colour nonfiction books, poetry collections and a range of classics, there are texts to suit all readers and their capabilities.

New titles are added regularly with audio for all lower level books.

## The Stadium

Compete in real time against students from around the country and around the world. These exciting head-to-head contests test skills in one of four areas—spelling, vocabulary, usage or grammar.

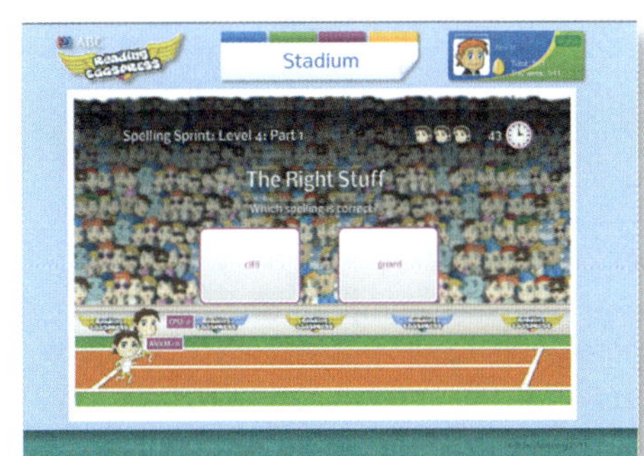

# Reading Eggspress Workbooks and the Australian Curriculum

Each workbook lesson focuses on a core comprehension strategy or key concept in grammar. The texts, strategies and concepts were developed to align with the Australian Curriculum.

## Year 2 Literacy

### Analysing, interpreting and evaluating

**AC9E2LY03** identify the purpose and audience of imaginative, informative and persuasive texts

**AC9E2LY04** read texts with phrasing and fluency, using phonic and word knowledge, and monitoring meaning by re-reading and self-correcting

**AC9E2LY05** use comprehension strategies such as visualising, predicting, connecting, summarising, monitoring and questioning to build literal and inferred meaning

## Year 2 Language

### Language for interaction

**AC9E2LA02** explore how language can be used for appreciating texts and providing reasons for preferences

### Text structure and organisation

**AC9E2LA04** understand how texts are made cohesive by using personal and possessive pronouns and by omitting words that can be inferred

### Language for expressing and developing ideas

**AC9E2LA06** understand that connections can be made between ideas by using a compound sentence with 2 or more independent clauses usually linked by a coordinating conjunction

**AC9E2LA07** understand that in sentences nouns may be extended into noun groups using articles and adjectives, and verbs may be expressed as verb groups

**AC9E2LA10** recognise that capital letters are used in titles and commas are used to separate items in lists

## Reading Eggspress Comprehension Strategy Overview

| Comprehension | Strategy | Fiction Lessons | Nonfiction Lesson |
|---|---|---|---|
| ***Literal***<br>Looks for explicitly stated answers in the texts. Answers **Who**, **What**, **When** and **Where** questions. | Think Marks | 21, 34, 41 | 26 |
| | Finding Facts and Information | 22 | 47 |
| | Main Idea and Details | 24, 25, 33, 44, 45, 55 | 28 |
| | Sequencing Events | | 29, 30, 36, 46, 58 |
| ***Inferential***<br>Finds implied information in the text. Looks for **text clues** and evidence that point to the correct answer. | Compare and Contrast | | 27, 37, 38, 48, 57, 59 |
| | Drawing Conclusions | 52 | |
| | Making Inferences | 23, 31, 42, 51 | 40, 50, 60 |
| | Making Predictions | 53 | |
| ***Critical***<br>Asks for **connections** or **opinions** on information in the text. Uses text clues to support the connections. | Making Connections | | 39 |
| | Visualisation | 32, 35, 43, 54 | 49, 56 |

## Reading Eggspress Grammar Overview

| Grammar | Focus | Fiction Lessons | Nonfiction Lesson |
|---|---|---|---|
| ***Sentence***<br>Looks at how **clauses** are structured and how they come together to **build** cohesive sentences. | Common and Proper Nouns | 1 | |
| | Adjectives | | 2 |
| | Noun-pronoun Agreement | 3 | |
| | Compound Sentences | 5 | |
| | Action Verbs | 7 | |
| | Subject-verb Agreement | | 8 |
| ***Text***<br>Assesses paragraph **composition** to see how sentences work together to create cohesive texts. | Time Connectives | | 6 |
| ***Punctuation***<br>Models correct punctuation **usage** for different types of words, clauses and sentences. | Commas | | 4 |

# STUDENT RECORD SHEET

Use this page to record the number of questions you answered correctly for each lesson.

## Term 1

| | | | | | | | |
|---|---|---|---|---|---|---|---|
| **Map 5** Fiction Lessons 440L–480L | **21** Think Marks | **22** Finding Facts and Information | **23** Making Inferences | **24** Main Idea and Details | **25** Main Idea and Details | **Grammar 1** Common and Proper Nouns | |
| | | | | | | | |
| **Map 6** Nonfiction Lessons 460L–520L | **26** Finding Facts and Information | **27** Compare and Contrast | **28** Main Idea and Details | **29** Sequencing Events | **30** Sequencing Events | **Grammar 2** Adjectives | **Assessment 1** *Ringing Guzzler* |
| | | | | | | | |

## Term 2

| | | | | | | | |
|---|---|---|---|---|---|---|---|
| **Map 7** Fiction Lessons 480L–520L | **31** Making Inferences | **32** Visualisation | **33** Main Idea and Details | **34** Think Marks | **35** Visualisation | **Grammar 3** Noun-pronoun Agreement | |
| | | | | | | | |
| **Map 8** Nonfiction Lessons 520L–560L | **36** Sequencing Events | **37** Compare and Contrast | **38** Compare and Contrast | **39** Making Connections | **40** Making Inferences | **Grammar 4** Commas | **Assessment 2** *Dolphins and Porpoises* |
| | | | | | | | |

## Term 3

| | | | | | | | |
|---|---|---|---|---|---|---|---|
| **Map 9** Fiction Lessons 520L–580L | **41** Think Marks | **42** Making Inferences | **43** Visualisation | **44** Main Idea and Details | **45** Main Idea and Details | **Grammar 5** Compound Sentences | |
| | | | | | | | |
| **Map 10** Nonfiction Lessons 560L–600L | **46** Sequencing Events | **47** Finding Facts and Information | **48** Compare and Contrast | **49** Visualisation | **50** Making Inferences | **Grammar 6** Time Connectives | **Assessment 3** *Ming Ming's Adventure* |
| | | | | | | | |

## Term 4

| | | | | | | | |
|---|---|---|---|---|---|---|---|
| **Map 11** Fiction Lessons 600L–620L | **51** Making Inferences | **52** Drawing Conclusions | **53** Making Predictions | **54** Visualisation | **55** Main Idea and Details | **Grammar 7** Action Verbs | |
| | | | | | | | |
| **Map 12** Nonfiction Lessons 620L–640L | **56** Visualisation | **57** Compare and Contrast | **58** Sequencing Events | **59** Compare and Contrast | **60** Making Inferences | **Grammar 8** Subject-verb Agreement | **Assessment 4** *Birds in Our Gardens* |
| | | | | | | | |

LESSON 21

# Go, Go Gecko

### Think Marks

To help us understand what we are reading, we can use **special marks**. These help us clearly see the parts we don't understand, and our connections to the text.

*I can see this part*

*What's this word?*

*I understand this part*

## Read the passage.

Use 👀 for parts of the story you can see.

Use a W for words you didn't know the meaning of.

Place a ✓ next to the part of the story you understand.

### The Chalk Box

The chalk box moves! The class gasps. Just a tiny gasp each, but together it makes the sound of a gust of wind.

Mr Mooney turns around. We're sitting quietly, so there's nothing he can say.

Mr Mooney turns back to the board. We go back to staring at the chalk box.

## Circle the correct answer.

1. **What** are the children watching?
   - a Mr Mooney
   - b chalk box
   - c gust of wind
   - d board
2. **Who** is sitting quietly?
   - a the class
   - b the gecko
   - c Mr Mooney
   - d the principal
3. **What** is moving?
   - a the chalk box
   - b the wind
   - c the board
   - d the class
4. **What** is a *gasp*?
   - a the sound of the wind
   - b a quick intake of breath
5. Which word could replace *turns* in this story?
   - a spins
   - b pushes
   - c circles
   - d shows



**ACELY1670** Use comprehension strategies to build literal meaning

## Read the passage.

**Use Think Marks to help you understand the passage.**

### A Gecko on the Teacher!

The gecko jumps onto Mr Mooney's hand. It runs up his arm. It leaps onto his head and waves at us.

Mr Mooney's eyes roll up and his mouth is the shape of an O.

His arms freeze halfway to his head, as if he's too afraid to move.

Box **what** Mr Mooney's face looks like

Underline **where** the gecko climbs

6 **What** is the gecko doing?

7 **How** does Mr Mooney feel?

8 Write about a time when you were were really surprised by something.

LESSON 22

# Tim's Money Tree

## Finding Facts and Information

To find facts and information in a text, we usually ask the questions **Who? What? Where?** or **When?** The answers can be clearly seen in the text.

## Read the passage.

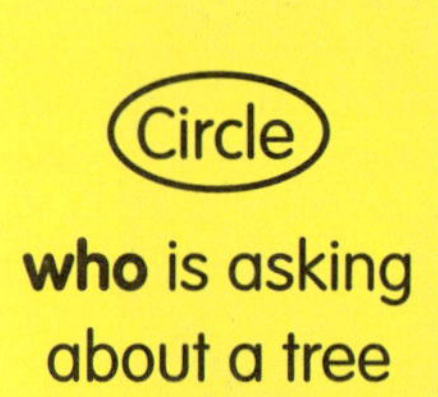

Box **what** the flowers grow into

Circle **who** is asking about a tree

Underline **what** type of tree Tim is asking about

**Colour** **where** to plant the tree

### A Good Idea

"Haven't you ever seen a money tree?" asked Mandy.

Tim shook his head. "How do people get a money tree?"

"Easy!" Mandy laughed. "They plant a coin in a pot full of dirt. Then they water it."

"When the coin grows into a tree, flowers grow on it. The flowers turn into money," she told him.

## Circle the correct answer.

1 **Who** is explaining the money tree?

a Mandy  b Tim  c Mum  d Sam

2 **What** is the first step to grow a money tree?

a Prune the tree.  b Plant a coin.
c Water the plant.  d Pick the flowers.

3 **Where** do you plant a money tree?

a in the forest  b next to a bank
c in a pot  d by a lake

**ACELY1670** Use comprehension strategies to build literal meaning

## Read the passage.

who was playing tricks

Box what Mandy needed to do

### Trouble!

Mum didn't like Mandy playing tricks on Tim.

"There's only one thing to do," Mum said. "Take the coins out of your piggybank and stick them on Tim's tree."

"But I was saving up to buy a book!" Mandy told her.

Underline

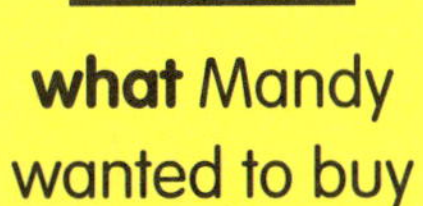

what Mandy wanted to buy

4 **Who** was playing tricks? ______________________

5 **What** does Mum want Mandy to do? ______________________

______________________

6 **Why** must Mandy do this? ______________________

______________________

7 **What** had Mandy been saving for? ______________________

**ACELY1670** Use comprehension strategies to build literal meaning

LESSON 23

# Songbird

**Making Inferences**

To make inferences while reading, we have to use clues in the text.

The clues help us find the answers that are hiding in the text.

## Read the passage.

Circle **who** was in the park

Box **what** the birds did at the park

### Happy Birds

Lots of cages hung in the trees. Grandpa hung Yan's cage with the others.

There were lots of grandpas and lots of songbirds. All the birds whistled.

The air was full of whistles. Grandpa sat on a bench and whistled too.

Yan liked to sing with the other birds. Grandpa liked to whistle with the other grandpas.

Underline **where** the cages hung

Colour **what** the grandpas did at the park

## Circle the correct answer.

1 **How** did the birds feel about going to the park?

a scared  b angry  c confused  d happy

2 Which **clues** tell you this?

a Lots of cages hung in the trees.  b Yan liked to sing with the other birds.

c All the birds whistled.  d Grandpa hung Yan's cage.

3 What **inference** can we make about the birds?

a Birds sing when they are happy.  b Birds like being in cages at the park.

c Birds are good for grandpas.  d Birds shouldn't be kept in cages.



**ACELY1670** Makes valid inferences using information in a text and students' own prior knowledge

## Read the passage.

Underline **what** Ling wants

Dear Grandpa,

The birds in Australia have bright feathers. Some are grey and pink. Others are white and wear yellow hats. They all sing very loudly.

I wish you could hear the birds, Grandpa. They are happy birds. I am sure Yan would be happy in Australia. You would be happy too.

I miss going to the park with you, Grandpa.

Love, Ling

Box **how** the birds sing

Colour **what** Ling misses

4 **How** do we know Ling likes Australian birds?

5 Does Ling want her Grandpa to come to Australia? How do we know?

LESSON 24

# Miss Feline's Unusual Pets

**Finding the Main Idea**

The main idea of a text is its key point. It sums up what the text is about.

Details in the text can help us find the main idea.

## Read the passage.

Box
Stella's **dialogue**

Underline
**how** the goose came through the window

Colour
**what** made Stella yell

### More Unusual Pets

A goose flew in through the window. She landed with a thump. She grumbled as she got up off the floor.

Then a hyena came to the door. He had the hiccups. He saw the goose and laughed.

They began to argue. It went on and on until Stella yelled, "Stop!"

The room was silent. The crocodile stood very still.

## Circle the correct answer/s.

1. What is the **main idea** of the text?
   - a Stella has ordinary pets.
   - b Stella doesn't want the animals to fight.
   - c Stella is excited.
   - d Stella is angry with the goose.

2. Which two sentences **support** the **main idea**?
   - a A goose flew in through the window. She landed with a thump.
   - b Then a hyena came to the door. He had the hiccups.
   - c They began to argue. It went on and on until Stella yelled, "Stop!"
   - d The room was silent. The crocodile stood very still.

# Read the passage.

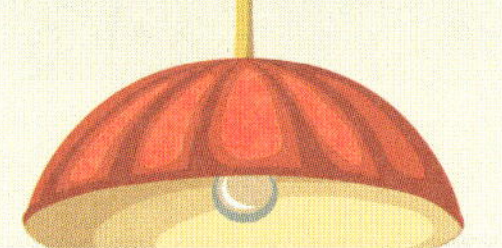

**Circle** the rabbit's **dialogue**

**Box** **how** the lion **felt**

## Rabbit Chase

"Help! Help!" yelled the rabbit. "The lion is trying to eat me!"

"I am not," said the lion. He sounded hurt. "I was trying to whisper in your ear. But one of your whiskers tickled my nose. I just slipped.

"Then your foot was in my mouth. I don't know how that happened. Mmmmmm, yummy."

**Underline** the lion's **dialogue**

**Colour** the **clue** that the lion was tasting the rabbit

3 Fill in the missing words.

The main idea of the text is that the ______________________

tried to eat the ___________________________.

4 Which **two details** helped you find the **main idea**?

a *The rabbit says,* ______________________________

______________________________

b *The lion says,* ______________________________

______________________________

LESSON 25

# The Ant and the Dove

### Finding the Main Idea

The main idea of a text is its key point. It sums up what the text is about. Details in the text can help us find the main idea.

## Read the passage.

Circle the **adjective** that describes the water

Box **what** the dove did with the leaf

A thirsty ant came to the edge of a river to get a drink. The fast-moving water splashed the ant and knocked it into the river. The ant was in trouble! It tried to swim but it was drowning.

A dove sitting in a tree picked a leaf and dropped it in the river, near the ant. The ant climbed onto the leaf and floated to safety on the bank of the river.

Underline **what** the water did to the ant

## Circle the correct answer/s.

1. Which **best** describes the main idea of the text?
   - a A dove saved an ant.
   - b An ant fell in the water.
   - c An ant was thirsty.
   - d A dove was flying by the river.

2. Which **two details support** the **main idea**?
   - a The water was moving quickly.
   - b Ants aren't good swimmers.
   - c A dove dropped a leaf in the river.
   - d The leaf floated to safety.

3. Which **best** describes the dove's actions?
   - a excited
   - b kind
   - c worried
   - d angry



**ACELY1670** Use comprehension strategies to build literal meaning

# Read the passage.

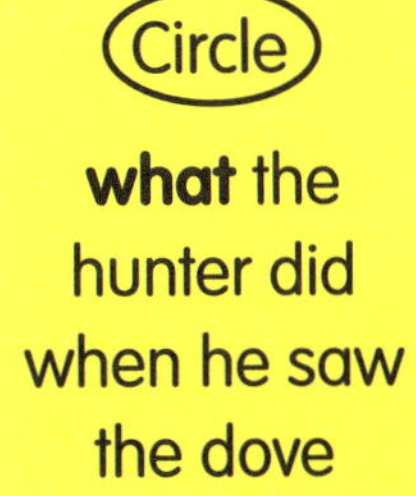


Box
**why** the dove flew away

Underline
**what** the ant did to the hunter

A little while later, a hunter came to the edge of the river. He saw the dove sitting in the tree and quickly drew his bow and aimed at the resting bird. The ant saw what was about to happen. It ran over to the hunter and bit his toe as hard as it could. The hunter cried out and dropped his bow. The dove was startled and flew away to safety.

4 Fill in the missing words.

This text is about how the ______________________

saved the ______________________.

5 Which **two details** helped you find the **main idea**?

a The ant ______________________

______________________

b The hunter ______________________

______________________

# Common and Proper Nouns

**Common nouns** name people, places and things. For example: **girl**, **boy**, **house**, **dog**. **Proper nouns** name specific people, places and things. They always start with a capital letter. For example: **Min**, **Sam**, **Mr Jackson**, **Australia**.

## Read the extract.

Circle the **names** of three **people**.

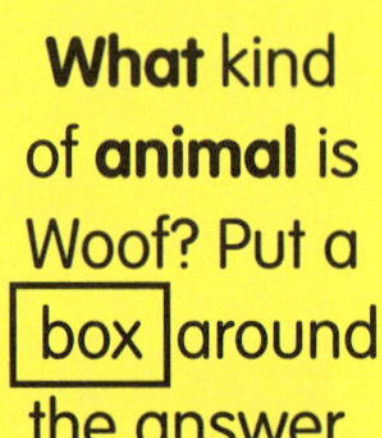

**What** kind of **animal** is Woof? Put a box around the answer.

**Highlight** the **name** of a **place**.

**What** kind of **animal** is Big Ears? Underline the answer.

### By the Nose

Sophie and Alice helped Harry back across the road.

Harry sneezed loudly.

"I smell cats — lots and lots of cats! And I smell Mrs Barker's dog, Woof. Woof smells like he has just had a bath."

"Yes, he has," said Mrs Barker. "And he didn't like it one bit."

Harry kept following his nose down Larkin Street. He named lots of flowers and trees, just by their smell. Sophie and Alice were amazed.

When Harry got to the end of the street, he took a big sniff.

"We are outside your house, Sophie," said Harry. "I can smell your rabbit, Big Ears."

**In each list, circle the common noun.**

1. a Sophie b Alice c cats d Woof
2. a Harry b Big Ears c Larkin Street d nose

**In each list, circle the proper noun.**

3. a Mrs Barker b flowers c trees d street
4. a rabbit b house c Harry d smell
5. a Woof b dog c cats d sniff



**ACELA1465** Recognise that capital letters signal proper nouns
**ACELA1468** Understand that nouns represent people, places and concrete objects

**6** **Draw lines to match the columns.**

| | |
|---|---|
| bus | place |
| baby | animal |
| monkey | thing |
| museum | person |

**7** **Label these common nouns.**

← ____________________

← ____________________

**8** **In the following pairs, circle the common noun and colour the proper noun.**

| | | |
|---|---|---|
| river<br>Amazon | Victoria<br>girl | month<br>April |
| boy<br>William | Snowball<br>cat | Ford<br>car |

**9** **Complete each sentence with a noun from the box.**

**a** "I can smell my way around Larkin ____________________," said Harry.

**b** "I can smell chocolate ____________________," said Harry.

**c** "I can smell Mogs the ____________________ above me," said Harry.

**d** Sophie and ____________________ could see Mrs Jolly in the kitchen.

**e** Mrs Jolly was lifting a ____________________ of biscuits from the ____________________.

| **biscuits** | **Alice** | **Street** | **oven** | **cat** | **tray** |
|---|---|---|---|---|---|

**ACELA1465** Recognise that capital letters signal proper nouns
**ACELA1468** Understand that nouns represent people, places and concrete objects

LESSON 26

# Summer

**Finding Facts and Information**

To find facts and information in a text, we usually ask the questions **Who? What? Where?** or **When?** The answers can be clearly seen in the text.

## Read the passage.

Circle **what** flowers make in summer

Box **what** covers trees in summer

Colour **what** happens to fruit in summer

Underline **what** happens to tree trunks in summer

### Plants in Summer

*Plants grow quickly in summer.*

Many plants flower in summer. Flowers make seeds. Some flowers, like apple blossoms, become fruit. Fruit grows and ripens in the summer.

In summer, trees are covered in green leaves. The leaves make food for the tree. The trunk grows thicker.

## Circle the correct answer.

1. **When** do apple blossoms become fruit?
   a summer b spring c winter d autumn
2. **What** do the leaves of a tree do in summer?
   a attract insects
   b make food for the tree
   c make roots
   d protect the trunk
3. **What** ripens in summer?
   a leaves b trees c fruit d flowers



**ACELY1670** Use comprehension strategies to build literal meaning

# Read the passage.

Circle summer **foods**

## Summer Food

*We eat more fresh food in summer.*

Salads are made from fresh summer vegetables. Families enjoy the outdoors by having picnics and barbeques.

Many fruits, such as berries, melons and peaches, are ripe in the summer. Fruit salad is good for you and tastes good too.

Underline summer **activities**

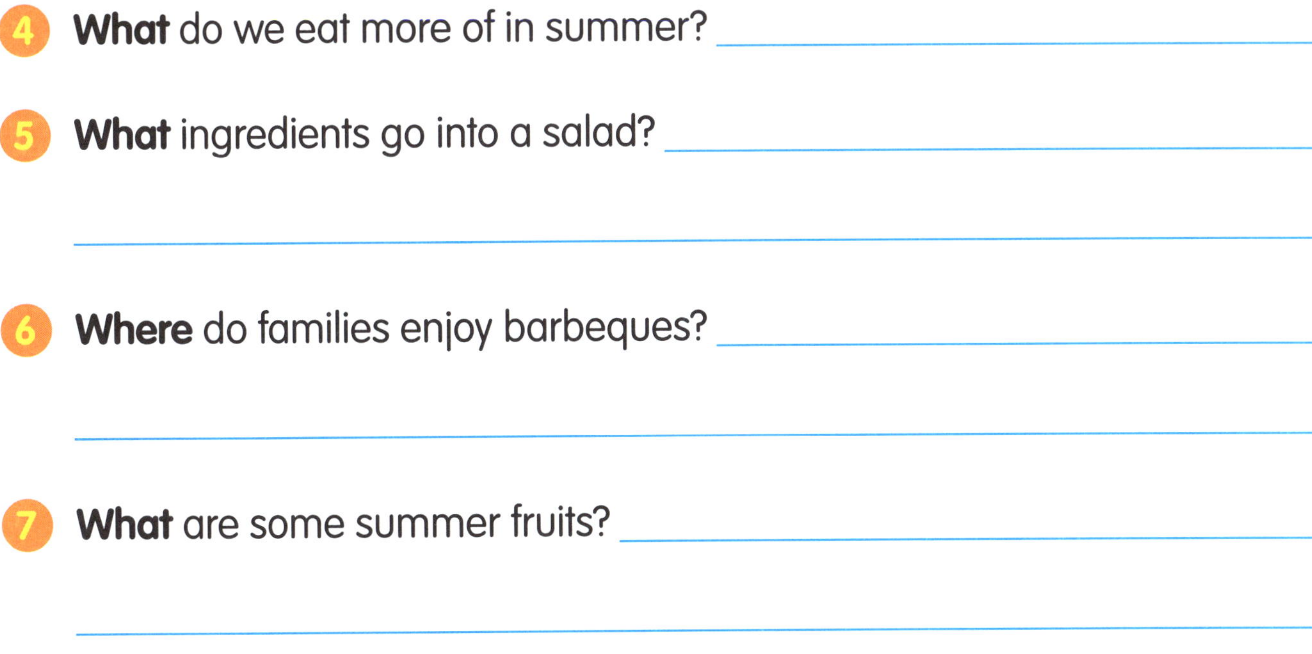

4 **What** do we eat more of in summer? ______________________

5 **What** ingredients go into a salad? ______________________

______________________

6 **Where** do families enjoy barbeques? ______________________

______________________

7 **What** are some summer fruits? ______________________

______________________

8 **What** can be made with summer fruits? ______________________

LESSON 27

# Dry

**Compare and Contrast**

When we compare and contrast information, we look for the similarities and differences between details in the text.

## Read the passage.

Box **what** is hard for all animals to find in a dry place

Circle **how** large mammals find water

Underline **how** bilbies and kangaroo rats get water

### Finding Water

*Water is hard to find in a dry habitat.*

Birds and large mammals, such as antelopes, elephants and zebras, travel long distances to find water.

Other animals get water from the food they eat. Bilbies and kangaroo rats get water from insects, fruit, seeds and leaves.

1 Put a [✔] next to information that is true. Put a [✗] next to information that is false.

a [ ] Antelopes and elephants are mammals.

b [ ] It is hard for all animals to find water in a dry habitat.

c [ ] Zebras drink more water than any other animal.

d [ ] Bilbies and kangaroo rats are ocean animals.

e [ ] Fruit, seeds and leaves can give some animals water.

f [ ] Elephants are large mammals.

**ACELY1670** Use comprehension strategies to build inferred meaning

# Read the passage.

Box **what** special strategies all desert animals have

Colour **how** kangaroo rats and fennec foxes stay cool

Underline **how** reptiles stay cool

## Conserving Water

*Desert animals have special water-saving strategies.*

Some animals in dry habitats do not sweat to cool down. This helps the kangaroo rat and the fennec fox to conserve water.

Reptiles have thick skins. Spiders and insects have exoskeletons. These hard, outer shells reduce water loss.

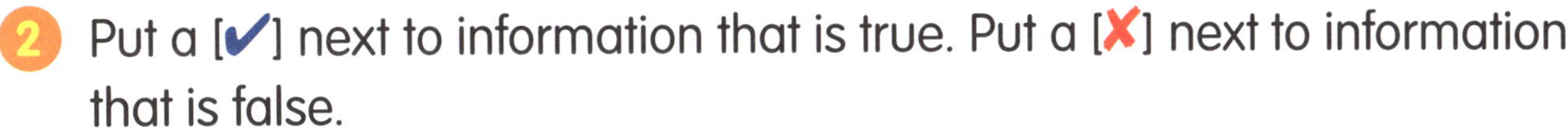

**2** Put a [✔] next to information that is true. Put a [✘] next to information that is false.

- **a** [ ] The fennec fox does not sweat to help it cool down.
- **b** [ ] All desert animals have ways to conserve water.
- **c** [ ] Kangaroo rats have thick skins to help them save water.
- **d** [ ] Spiders have exoskeletons to keep cool.
- **e** [ ] Desert animals need to always be near water.
- **f** [ ] An exoskeleton can help an animal reduce water loss.

LESSON 28

# Trains

### Identifying the Main Idea

To discover what a text is about, you need to look for the main idea or key point.

Facts and details in the text can help you find the main idea.

## Read the passage.

Circle **which** trains were pulled by steam engines

Box **how** steam is made

Underline **what** steam engines burn

Colour **when** steam trains were used

### Old Trains

*The first trains were pulled along by steam engines.*

Steam engines burn coal. The burning coal heats water to make steam. The steam makes the wheels turn.

In the 1800s steam trains were a quick and cheap way to travel for fun as well as for work. Today most steam trains are for tourists.

## Circle the correct answer.

1 What is the **main idea** of the text?

a to give facts about why train travel is fun
b to describe how steam trains burn coal
c to explain how steam trains work and were used
d to tell others where to ride steam trains

2 Which two sentences best **support** the **main idea**?

a Today most steam trains are for tourists.
b The first trains were pulled along by steam engines.
c In the 1800s steam trains were a quick and easy way to travel.
d The steam makes the wheels turn.



**ACELY1670** Use comprehension strategies to build literal meaning

## Read the passage.

**Colour** **how** modern trains are powered

Box **where** new trains are used

### New Trains

*Today, most trains have diesel or electric engines.*

The new engines are quieter and cleaner than coal-powered steam engines. Diesel trains are often used in country areas. Many electric trains run in cities.

Some electric trains can travel very fast. They are called high-speed trains. The bullet trains in Japan can travel three times faster than a car.

Underline **features** of new trains

3 Fill in the missing words.

This text is about different types of ______________________.

4 Give **two details** that support the **main idea**.

a Most trains ______________________

______________________

b New train engines ______________________

______________________

LESSON 29

# Bread

**Sequencing Events**

To identify the sequence of events in a text, look at numbers and words that give clues to the order in which things happen.

## Read the passage.

### Growing Grain

*Wheat, oat, rye and rice are all grains. People eat more grain than any other food.*

Farmers grow wheat in large, flat fields. They use machines called cultivators to prepare the soil for planting.

Farmers mix fertiliser with seeds to help the grain grow. They then use a seeder to drop the seeds into furrows.

1. **Order** the events to grow grain.
   - ☐ Use a seeder to drop seeds.
   - ☐ Mix fertiliser with seeds.
   - ☐ Choose your grain.
   - ☐ Use a cultivator to prepare the soil for planting.
   - ☐ Choose a large, flat field.

2. Draw would need to happen **next** for the seeds to grow?

## Read the passage.

### Refining

*Trucks carry wheat to flour mills. The wheat grains are made into flour.*

People inspect the wheat to make sure it is good quality.

The grain is cleaned and soaked in water for 10 to 20 hours. This separates the outer layer of bran from the soft, inner part. Rollers crush the wheat into a powder called flour.

Circle **how** the wheat gets to the flour mills

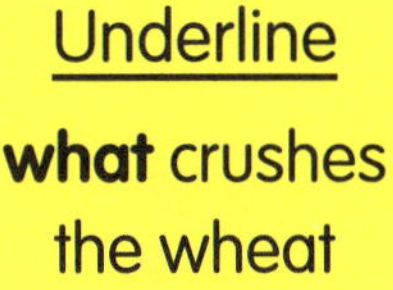

Underline **what** crushes the wheat

Box **how long** the grain is soaked

3 What happens to the wheat **before** it is soaked?

4 What happens to the wheat **after** it is soaked?

5 What does this text explain?

LESSON 30

# Cooking and Change

**Sequencing Events**

To identify the sequence of events in a text, look at numbers and words that give clues to the order in which things happen.

## Read the passage.

### Popcorn Recipe

1. Put the oil into the pot. Add the popping corn.
2. Cover the pot with a lid. Place the pot on the stove. Set the stove to medium heat.
3. Don't open the lid while the corn is popping. Turn off the heat when the popping stops.
4. Let the popcorn cool, and then eat.

1. What happens **before** you put the popping corn in the pot?

   a Heat the pot.
   b Fill the pot with warm water.
   c Add salt to the pot.
   d Put oil into the pot.

2. **Order** the events using the numbers 1-4.

   ☐ Pour the popcorn into a bowl and enjoy.
   ☐ Place the pot onto a medium heat.
   ☐ Gently move the pot off the burner.
   ☐ Put the oil and popping corn in the pot.



ACELY1670 Use comprehension strategies to build literal meaning

## Read the passage.

### Pancake Recipe

1. First ____________, whisk the eggs in a bowl and add the milk. Place the dry ingredients in a separate bowl.

2. ____________, pour the milk mixture into the flour. Stir until you have a smooth batter.

3. ____________, heat butter in the frying pan. Add a spoonful of batter to the pan.

4. ____________, cook until the bubbles pop. Flip the pancake over and cook until golden brown.

3 Add in **time adverbs** for the pancake recipe.

4 Draw the pancake recipe. Add step 5.

Step 1

Step 2

Step 3

Step 4

Step 5

**ACELY1670** Use comprehension strategies to build literal meaning

GRAMMAR LESSON 2

# Adjectives

**Adjectives** give information about **nouns** and **pronouns**. For example: **Tom is a tall boy. Ali has two cats. A kangaroo is an Australian animal.**

## Read the extract.

**What** kind of **time** is spring? Circle the answer.

**What** are the **days** like in spring? Put a box around the answer.

**What** days are **good** for flying kites? Highlight the answer.

**What** are **strawberries** like in spring? Colour the answers.

### People in Spring

People spend more time outside in spring.

Spring is an exciting time outdoors. There are many new plants and animals. The air smells fresh. The cold winter is over.

The early sunrise makes waking up easier. The longer days and warm sunshine give many people more energy.

Dandelions make seeds in spring. Children like to blow the seeds away.

Windy days are good for flying kites. Early mornings are good for fishing.

People enjoy eating fresh, spring fruits and vegetables after the cold winter. Strawberries are sweet and juicy in spring.

## In each sentence, find the adjective.

1. Spring is my favourite season.
   a Spring  b favourite  c my  d season
2. There are lots of new plants and animals to see in spring.
   a There  b lots  c new  d see
3. Dandelions make fluffy seeds in spring.
   a fluffy  b Dandelions  c spring  d seeds
4. On spring mornings, people get up early to go fishing.
   a spring  b mornings  c up  d fishing



ACELA1462 Identify language that can be used for appreciating texts and the qualities of people and things

## 5 Circle the adjectives that can describe the tree.

big icy green blue deep shady small leafy tall beautiful

## 6 Colour the adjective that correctly completes each sentence.

a There are (two, four) seasons in a year.

b In spring it gets (warmer, cooler).

c Summer is the (hottest, coldest) season.

d In winter the days are (long, short).

e People carry umbrellas if the weather is (clear, cloudy).

## 7 Write the adjectives under the correct heading.

blue twelve brown bitter sweet twenty purple seven spicy

| How many? | What colour? | What taste? |
|---|---|---|
| ______ | ______ | ______ |
| ______ | ______ | ______ |
| ______ | ______ | ______ |

## 8 Match the adjectives with similar meanings.

| | |
|---|---|
| colourful | freezing |
| icy | tasty |
| hungry | bright |
| delicious | starving |

ASSESSMENT 1:

# Ringing Guzzler

My dog eats everything. Yesterday he guzzled the sausages in Mum's shopping bag. Last week it was my homework.

This morning Mum couldn't find her mobile phone. She looked on the kitchen bench, in the car, next to the bed. It was nowhere to be seen.

"Okay," said Dad, "I'll use my mobile phone to call your phone."

Guzzler burped. Dad called the number. Yes! There was a faint ring. The sound was coming from somewhere near Guzzler. Oh, no! It was Guzzler! He'd guzzled Mum's phone.

Dad and I laughed, but Mum said, "We'll take Guzzler to the vet to get my phone back, but that's it! I'm going to give him away."

"No, Mum," I cried. "You can't give Guzzler away. He's mine!"

## Circle the correct answer.

1 Why is the dog called Guzzler? INFERENTIAL

a He likes sausages.

b His owner liked the name.

c He eats everything.

d He has a big belly.

2 What was in Mum's shopping bag? LITERAL

a a mobile phone

b sausages

c a tennis ball

d the writer's homework

3 Why couldn't Mum find her phone? LITERAL

a It was under the bed.
b It was in the car.
c It was in a kitchen drawer.
d It was inside Guzzler.

4 Which word is similar in meaning to *burped*? VOCABULARY

a coughed
b sneezed
c belched
d yawned

5 How did Mum know where her phone was? LITERAL

a She heard it ring.
b She remembered where she'd put it.
c She accidentally tripped over it.
d She saw it on the kitchen bench.

6 What did Dad and the narrator think when they found out what Guzzler had done? They thought it was … INFERENTIAL

a dangerous.
b funny.
c unfair.
d silly.

7 How did Mum feel about Guzzler eating her phone? INFERENTIAL

a worried
b confused
c amazed
d angry

8 Who will help Mum get her phone back? LITERAL

a the vet
b the doctor
c Dad
d the plumber

9 What does Mum plan to do with Guzzler? LITERAL

a sell him
b give him away
c make him stay outside
d lock him up

10 How does the narrator feel about Mum's decision? INFERENTIAL

a glad
b disappointed
c upset
d scared

LESSON 31

# Take Me to Your Leader

**Making Inferences**

To make inferences while reading, we have to use clues in the text.

The clues help us find the answers that are hiding in the text.

## Read the passage.

**Circle** the **alien's dialogue**

**Box** **adjectives** that describe the **alien**

**Underline** **how** Tim moves to the closet

**Colour** **Tim's dialogue**

**Thump! Thump! Thump!**

What is that?

"Thump!"

It's coming from the closet. Tim creeps over and slides the door open. A tiny purple alien steps out and pokes Tim on the foot.

"Take me to your weader!"

Tim jumps back on the bed. The alien is only as big as a teddy bear but he has a zap gun. The gun is pointed at Tim.

"Wha ... what?" Tim asks.

## Circle the correct answer.

1. **How** does Tim feel about the alien?

   a scared  b angry  c confused  d happy

2. Which **clue** tells you this?

   a "Thump!"  b "Take me to your weader!"
   c What is that?  d "Wha ... what?" Tim asks.

3. What **inference** can we make about Tim?

   a Tim is bigger than the alien.  b He has a very messy room.
   c Teddy bears are his favourite toys.  d He lives on a planet with aliens.



**ACELY1670** Makes valid inferences using information in a text and students' own prior knowledge

## Read the passage.

Circle words that describe **Gweep's appearance**

Box **Gweep's dialogue**

Underline **Tim's dialogue**

### Slime Jelly

"Here is some slime instead," Tim yells.

Gweep looks in the bowl. "This bad."

Tim looks at the yummy, wobbly, green jelly. "It's really very nice."

Tears form in Gweep's three round eyes. "It's saying no!"

"The slime isn't saying no. It's shaking because it's scared of you."

"Is it scared?" Gweep smiles. "Of me?"

4 **Why** does Tim call the jelly *slime*?

5 Do you think Gweep is happy at the end? How do you know?

**ACELY1670** Makes valid inferences using information in a text and students' own prior knowledge

LESSON 32

# Mandy Made Me Do It

## Visualisation

Good readers imagine pictures when they read a text. This is called visualising.

Looking for key words in the text helps us create images.

## Read the passage.

Circle the **noises** Tim made

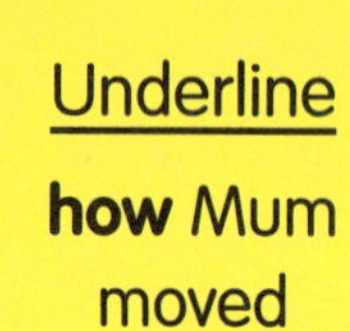

### Beds Are Not Trampolines

Tim did a star jump. Then he fell off the bed and landed on his nose. He started to cry.

He cried louder and louder. Mum came running into the room and picked him up.

"Now what have you done?" she asked, looking at his red nose.

"Mandy made me do it," Tim sobbed.

## Circle the correct answer.

1. **How** was Tim feeling?
   - a scared
   - b nervous
   - c excited
   - d sad

2. Which **key words** tell what Tim did?
   - a running into the room
   - b landed on his nose

3. Which word helps us **hear** how Tim was feeling?
   - a landed
   - b sobbed
   - c nose
   - d fell

4. Which word helps us **see** Tim's nose?
   - a landed
   - b jump
   - c cry
   - d red



**ACELY1670** Makes valid inferences using information in a text and students' own prior knowledge

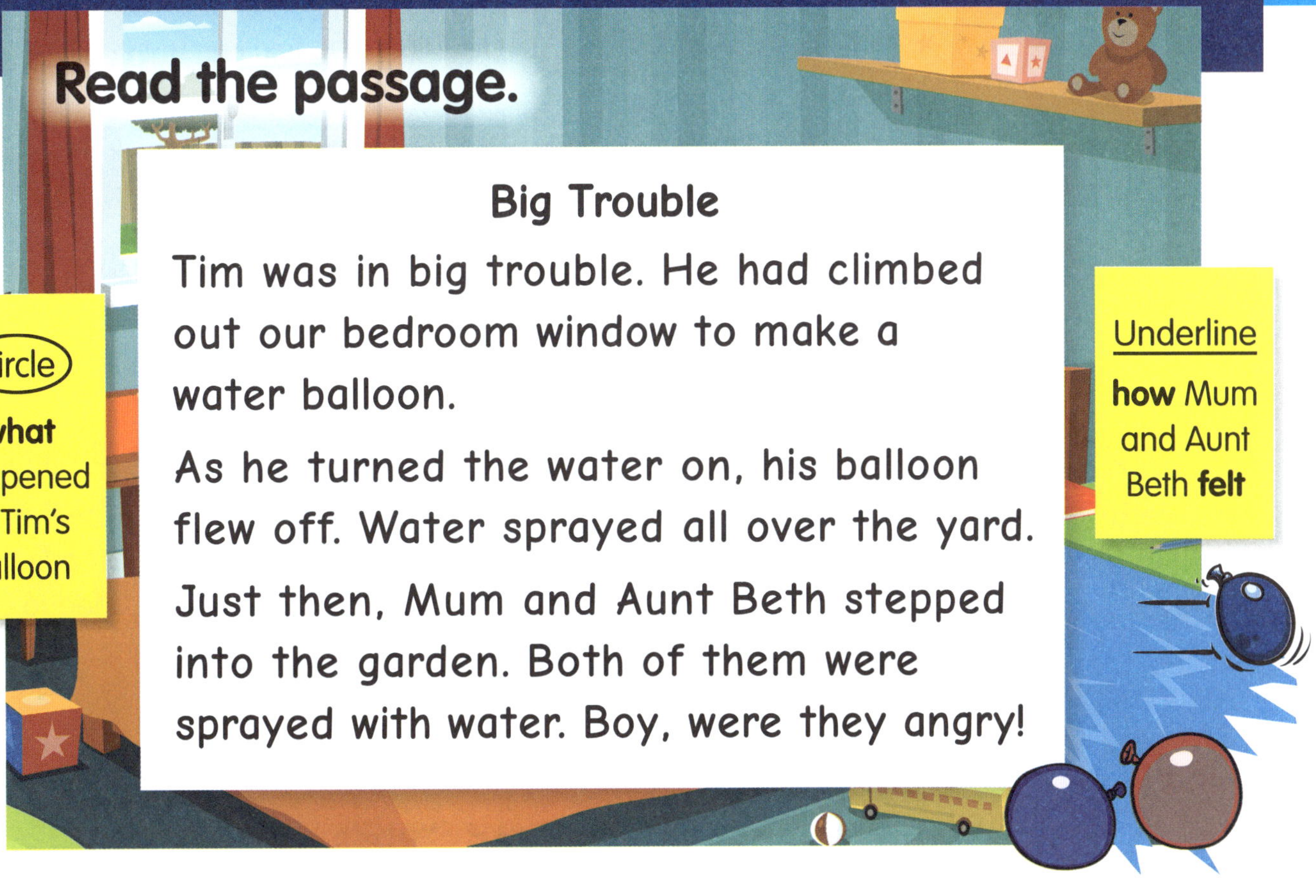

## Read the passage.

### Big Trouble

Tim was in big trouble. He had climbed out our bedroom window to make a water balloon.

As he turned the water on, his balloon flew off. Water sprayed all over the yard.

Just then, Mum and Aunt Beth stepped into the garden. Both of them were sprayed with water. Boy, were they angry!

Circle **what** happened to Tim's balloon

Underline **how** Mum and Aunt Beth **felt**

5 Imagine if you turned on water and it sprayed on you. How would you feel?

6 Draw Tim's **actions** from the text.

7 Re-read the story. Draw Tim, Mum and Aunt Beth's faces at the end.

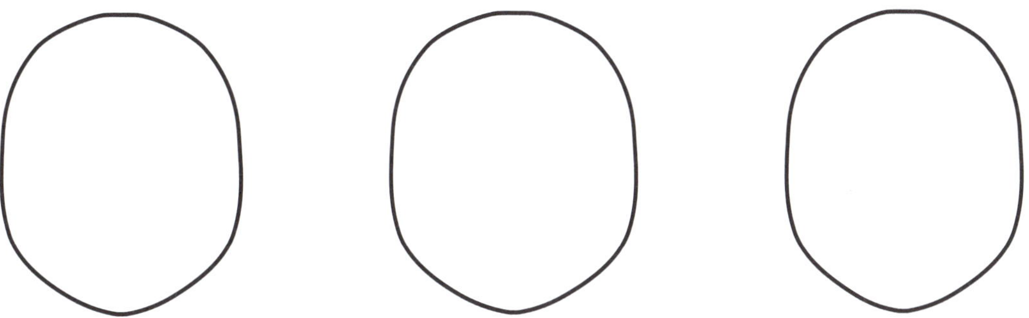

**ACELY1670** Makes valid inferences using information in a text and students' own prior knowledge

LESSON 33

# Saving Greedy Guts

**Finding the Main Idea**

The main idea of a text is its key point. It sums up what the text is about.

Details in the text can help us find the main idea.

## Read the passage.

Circle the **verbs** about **eating**

### Gee-Gee?

When I picked him up, Greedy Guts chewed on my fingers. Then he gnawed the strap of my watch.

I put him on the floor and he untied my shoelaces. Then he tried to pull my left sock off. He loved me so much, he wanted to eat me. How could I resist him?

"Mum, please," I begged. "He's perfect."

Underline the **things** Greedy Guts tried to **eat**

## Circle the correct answer/s.

1. Find the **main idea** of the text.
   - a Greedy Guts was bought from a pet shop.
   - b Greedy Guts is perfect.
   - c Greedy Guts likes to eat everything.
   - d Greedy Guts wants to wear socks.
2. Which **two** sentences best **support** the main idea?
   - a "Mum, please," I begged. "He's perfect."
   - b We bought Greedy Guts at a pet shop.
   - c When I picked him up, Greedy Guts chewed on my fingers.
   - d Then he gnawed the strap of my watch.
   - e He loved me so much, he wanted to eat me. How could I resist him?



**ACELY1670** Use comprehension strategies to build literal meaning

## Read the passage.

Circle **who** sent the jacket

**Colour** **what** the jacket looked like

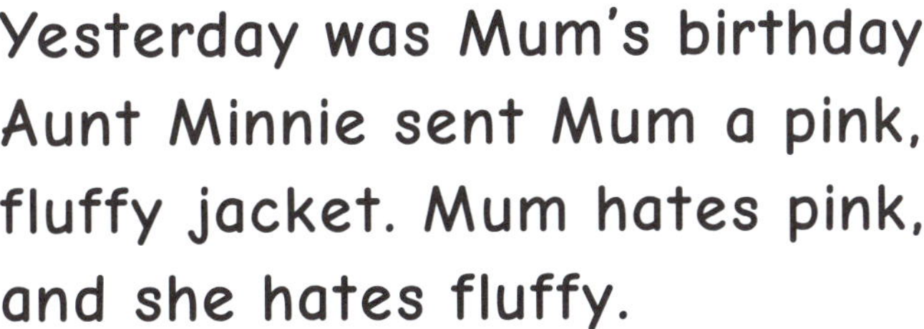

Yesterday was Mum's birthday. Aunt Minnie sent Mum a pink, fluffy jacket. Mum hates pink, and she hates fluffy.

"I must ring her to say thank you," Mum said. "Aunt Minnie is a dear to remember my birthday, even if she doesn't remember what I like," Mum said.

"Aunt Minnie is family, and you can't choose your family. Mmmm ... perhaps I could wash it and say that it shrank."

Underline **why** Mum got the jacket

**3** Fill in the missing words.

The text is about what ______________________ thinks of

______________________________ present.

**4** Which **two details** helped you find the main idea?

a Mum hates ______________________

______________________________

b Mum says, ______________________

______________________________

LESSON 34

# The Courtship of the Yonghy-Bonghy-Bo

## Think Marks

The Yonghy-Bonghy-Bo is a nonsense poem. It tries to make us laugh. To help us understand the poem, we can use **special marks**. These help us clearly see the parts we don't understand, and the connections we make to the text.

*I can see this part*

*What's this word?*

*I understand this part*

## Read the passage.

Use [eyes] for parts of the story you can see.

Use a W for words you didn't know the meaning of.

Place a ✓ next to the part of the poem you understand

### The Courtship of the Yonghy-Bonghy-Bo

On the coast of Coromandel
Where the early pumpkins blow,
In the middle of the woods
Lived the Yonghy-Bonghy-Bo.
Two chairs, and half a candle,
One old jug without a handle —
These were all his wordly goods:
In the middle of the woods,
These were all the worldly goods
Of the Yonghy-Bonghy-Bo,
Of the Yonghy-Bonghy-Bo.

## Circle the correct answer.

1 **Where** does the Yonghy-Bonghy-Bo live?

- a in an old jar
- b inside a small pumpkin
- c in a jug
- d in the middle of the woods

2 **What** does *worldly goods* mean?

______________________________

______________________________

# Read the passage.

## Use Think Marks to help you understand the passage.

Box the word that **rhymes** with Yonghy-Bonghy-bo

Circle words that describe the **area** around the Yonghy-Bonghy-Bo's home

### The Courtship of the Yonghy-Bonghy-Bo

On the coast of Coromandel
Where the early pumpkins blow,
In the middle of the woods
Lived the Yonghy-Bonghy-Bo.
Two chairs, and half a candle,
One old jug without a handle —
These were all his wordly goods:
In the middle of the woods,
These were all the worldly goods
Of the Yonghy-Bonghy-Bo,
Of the Yonghy-Bonghy-Bo.

3 Draw a map of the area where the Yonghy-Bonghy-Bo lives.

LESSON 35

# The Dog and His Reflection

**Visualisation**

Good readers imagine pictures when they read a text. This is called visualising.

Looking for key words in the text helps us create the images.

## Read the passage.

Circle words that **describe** the **bone**

Box **where** the dog was going

A dog had a fresh, meaty bone, which a butcher had thrown to him. He was heading home with his wonderful bone, as fast as he could go.

Underline **who** gave the dog the bone

## Circle the correct answer.

1. **What** did the butcher throw?
   a a bone b a biscuit c a treat d a ball
2. Which **key word** describes the dog's feelings about the bone?
   a fast b wonderful c butcher d thrown
3. Which two words help us **visualise** the bone?
   a butcher b meaty c wonderful d fresh
4. Which words help us **visualise** the dog's speed?
   a wonderful bone b meaty bone
   c thrown to him d as fast as he could go



**ACELT1587** Discuss moral stories from varied cultures to identify and compare their central messages

## Read the passage.

As the dog crossed a bridge over a pond, he looked down and saw himself reflected in the quiet water. The image was like looking in a mirror.

But the dog thought he saw a real dog carrying another bone—a bone much bigger than his! Without thinking, the dog dropped his bone and leaped at the dog in the pond.

what the **dog saw**

Underline a word that **describes the water**

5. **Where** did the dog see himself?
   - a the ocean
   - b a waterfall
   - c a pond
   - d a swimming pool

6. Which words helped you visualise the water?

   ______________________________

7. **What** did the dog see?
   - a a mirror
   - b a bigger dog
   - c a bigger bone
   - d his reflection

8. Where can you see your own reflection?

   ______________________________

9. What would the dog's reflection have looked like in the water?

   ______________________________

GRAMMAR LESSON 3

# Noun–pronoun Agreement

**Pronouns** stand in place of nouns. They save us repeating nouns. For example: **Jack put on Jack's hat. Jack put on his hat.** Pronouns must agree with the nouns they refer to.

## Read the extract.

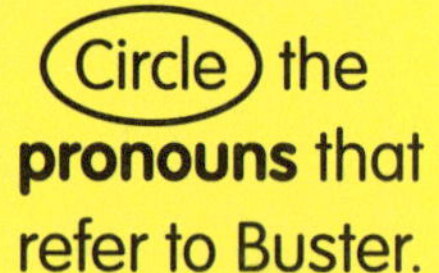

Circle the **pronouns** that refer to Buster.

Put a box around the **pronouns** that refer to the blow up seal.

Highlight the **pronouns** that refer to Buster.

Underline the **pronouns** that refer to Holly.

**Bubble Buster**

Buster loved pool parties. He could jump and bomb. He could splash and muck about.

He jumped on Holly's blow up seal. The seal burst. It hissed as it sped across the pool.

"Wow!" said Buster. But Holly didn't think it was funny. Her seal looked like an old plastic bag.

Buster dived under the water when his father pointed an angry finger at him.

Buster saw Holly playing with her bubble maker. As she made bubble after bubble, he began to chase them. Soon he was popping all the bubbles. He liked hearing them pop.

"I'm the bubble buster!" he shouted.

## Circle the correct pronoun to fill each gap.

1. When Buster landed on the seal, ______ burst.
   a it  b its  c they  d him
2. Holly was cross with Buster when he jumped on ______ blow up seal.
   a she  b her  c hers  d him
3. Buster's father was also angry with ______.
   a he  b his  c him  d she
4. Buster popped the bubbles when ______ floated towards him.
   a he  b their  c them  d they



ACELA1464 Understand how texts are made cohesive through language features, including word associations

## 5 Complete each sentence with the correct pronoun.

a Holly and I are playing with ______________ bubble makers. **we our**

b Buster said the bubble maker was his, not ______________. **my mine**

c I told Buster he could play with ______________ bubble maker. **me my**

d Holly and Buster let ______________ play with their bubble makers. **us we**

e The bubble makers are ______________, not theirs. **our ours**

## 6 Replace the nouns in brackets with pronouns.

a Holly gave (Buster) ____________ the bubble maker.

b Holly told Buster not to break (the bubble maker) ____________.

c (Holly and Buster) ____________ liked pool parties and blowing bubbles.

d Everyone had fun at (Holly and Buster's) ______________ pool parties.

e Buster hurt (Buster's) ____________ arm when he fell into the flower bed.

f Buster promised (Buster) ____________ would look after the bubble maker.

## 7 In each sentence, put a circle around the pronoun. Underline the noun it refers to.

a Buster wanted to blow square bubbles, so he bent the ring.

b The wire broke when Buster bent it.

c Bubbles burst when they fly too high.

d Buster blinked when the bubbles hit his face.

e The children cried when their bubble maker broke.

LESSON 36

# From Farms to You

**Sequencing Events**

To identify the sequence of events in a text, look at numbers and words that give clues to the order in which things happen.

## Read the passage.

Circle **two ways** of harvesting berries

Underline what happens to the berries **before** they are cooked

### Berries to Jam

*Berries can be eaten fresh. They can also be cooked with sugar to make jam.*

1. Berries grow on small bushes or plants in fields and hothouses.
2. Some farmers use machines to harvest the ripe berries. Others are picked by hand.
3. The berries are washed, trimmed and cut up or mashed. Then, the berries are cooked with sugar until the mixture is thick.
4. Next, the hot jam is poured into jars and sealed to keep it fresh.

1. What happens to the berries **before** they are harvested?

2. What happens to the berries **after** they are washed and mashed?

3. Where is the jam poured **after** it is cooked?

4. What **text feature** tells you the steps must be done in order?

## Read the passage.

### Cows to Milk

First, the cows are taken to the milking shed.

__________, they are milked using milking machines.

__________, milk tankers take the milk to a factory where it is heated to kill any harmful bacteria.

__________, the milk is put into bottles or cartons and kept refrigerated.

__________, it is taken to shops and supermarkets.

5 Add in **time adverbs** to complete the passage.

6 Draw **the process** from cows in the milking shed to milk in the supermarket.

Step 1

Step 2

Step 3

Step 4

Step 5

Step 6

LESSON 37

# Tools

**Compare and Contrast**
Look for similarities and differences. This table compares and contrasts everyday tools we use.

## Read the table.

| Tool | Function | Powered by humans | Powered by electricity | Powered by battery |
|---|---|---|---|---|
| hammer | used to hammer nails, break rocks and remove nails | ✓ | ✗ | ✗ |
| pen | used to write | ✓ | ✗ | ✗ |
| blender | used to mix foods and liquids | ✗ | ✓ | ✗ |
| calculator | used to do maths | ✗ | ✗ | ✓ |

1. Put a [✓] next to information that is true. Put a [✗] next to information that is false.

   a ☐ Hammers and calculators are both powered by electricity.

   b ☐ You must have a battery to use a pen.

   c ☐ Batteries power calculators.

   d ☐ Pens and hammers are powered by humans.

   e ☐ A hammer and a pen have the same function.

   f ☐ Blenders are powered by electricity.

## Find the answer in the table.

2. Which tools are powered by humans? ______________________

3. Which tools are *not* powered by electricity? ______________________

4. Which tool is powered by battery? ______________________

5. Which tool is powered by electricity? ______________________



ACELY1670 Use comprehension strategies to build inferred meaning

## Read the passage.

**Colour** tools schools used **from** the 1970s

**Box** tools schools used **before** the 1970s

### 1970s

*Many new tools and gadgets became popular in the 1970s.*

Prior to the 1970s, most schools used books, blackboards, and paper as educational tools.

By the 1970s, many schools had film projectors, record players and tape recorders to help children learn.

By the late 1970s, people began to buy personal computers for their homes.

6 Complete the table using [✔] and [✘].

| School Tool | Used before 1970 | Used in the 1970s | Used today |
|---|---|---|---|
| Books | | | |
| Blackboards | | | |
| Paper and pencils | | | |
| Film projectors | | | |
| Record players | | | |
| Tape recorders | | | |

7 Which tools were used **before 1970**?

______________________________

8 Which tools were used before the 1970s and are **still used** in schools today?

______________________________

LESSON 38

# Transport

**Compare and Contrast**
Look for similarities and differences between details in the text.

Read the passage.

Underline the **purpose** of transport

Box types of **public transport**

Colour a **word** that means the same as **transport**

Circle types of **private transport**

## Transport

*Vehicles, such as cars, buses, trains, planes and boats, transport us from one place to another.*

Some people use transport to make short, daily trips to work or school. Others use it for longer journeys, such as a holiday or business trip overseas.

Public transport is designed for moving large groups of people. Buses, trains, trams, ferries and planes are types of public transport. Private transport includes cars, motorcycles and bicycles.

1 Complete the table about transport.

| | Purpose | Examples |
|---|---|---|
| Private transport | | |
| Public transport | | |

2 What does all transport do? ______________________________



ACELY1670 Use comprehension strategies to build inferred meaning

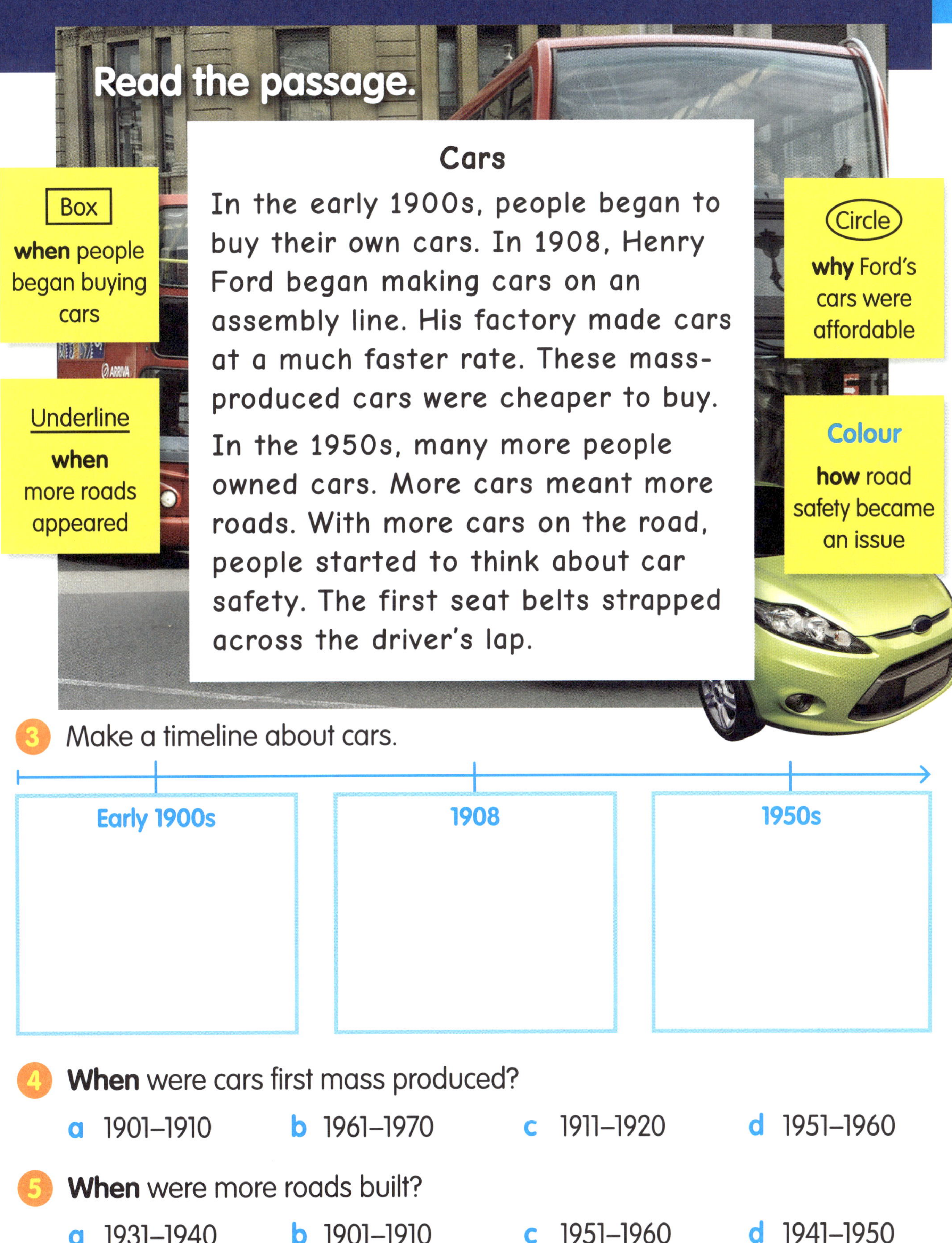

## Read the passage.

Box **when** people began buying cars

Underline **when** more roads appeared

Circle **why** Ford's cars were affordable

Colour **how** road safety became an issue

### Cars

In the early 1900s, people began to buy their own cars. In 1908, Henry Ford began making cars on an assembly line. His factory made cars at a much faster rate. These mass-produced cars were cheaper to buy.

In the 1950s, many more people owned cars. More cars meant more roads. With more cars on the road, people started to think about car safety. The first seat belts strapped across the driver's lap.

3 Make a timeline about cars.

| Early 1900s | 1908 | 1950s |
| --- | --- | --- |
| | | |

4 **When** were cars first mass produced?

a 1901–1910  b 1961–1970  c 1911–1920  d 1951–1960

5 **When** were more roads built?

a 1931–1940  b 1901–1910  c 1951–1960  d 1941–1950

LESSON 39

# Postcards

**Making Connections**

Good readers know how to make connections in a text. They can link words, ideas and events to themselves, things they have read, and real world events.

## Read the passage.

Underline **when** they went to the zoo

Box **what** they saw at the zoo

Colour **who** went to the zoo

Circle **what** they ate at the zoo

Dear Mum,

Today we got up really early and went to the zoo. It was huge! The giraffes had lots of room and the lions hid in the bushes. Dad pretended to be a mountain goat. We bought ice creams after lunch. Boo-boo had chocolate and I had vanilla. Dad carried us when we got really tired. See you tomorrow!

Love, T

xx

1. Draw a [link symbol] if you can **connect** with these ideas from the postcard.
   - a Today we got up really early.
   - b We went to the zoo.
   - c I saw giraffes and lions.
   - d Dad pretended to be a mountain goat.

2. **Share** with a friend **a story** of one of your connections.

   *Did the story happen to you?*

   *Did it happen in a book you read?*

   *Did you connect with the same or different ideas from the postcard?*



**ACELY1670** Makes connections between the text and students' own experiences and experiences with other texts

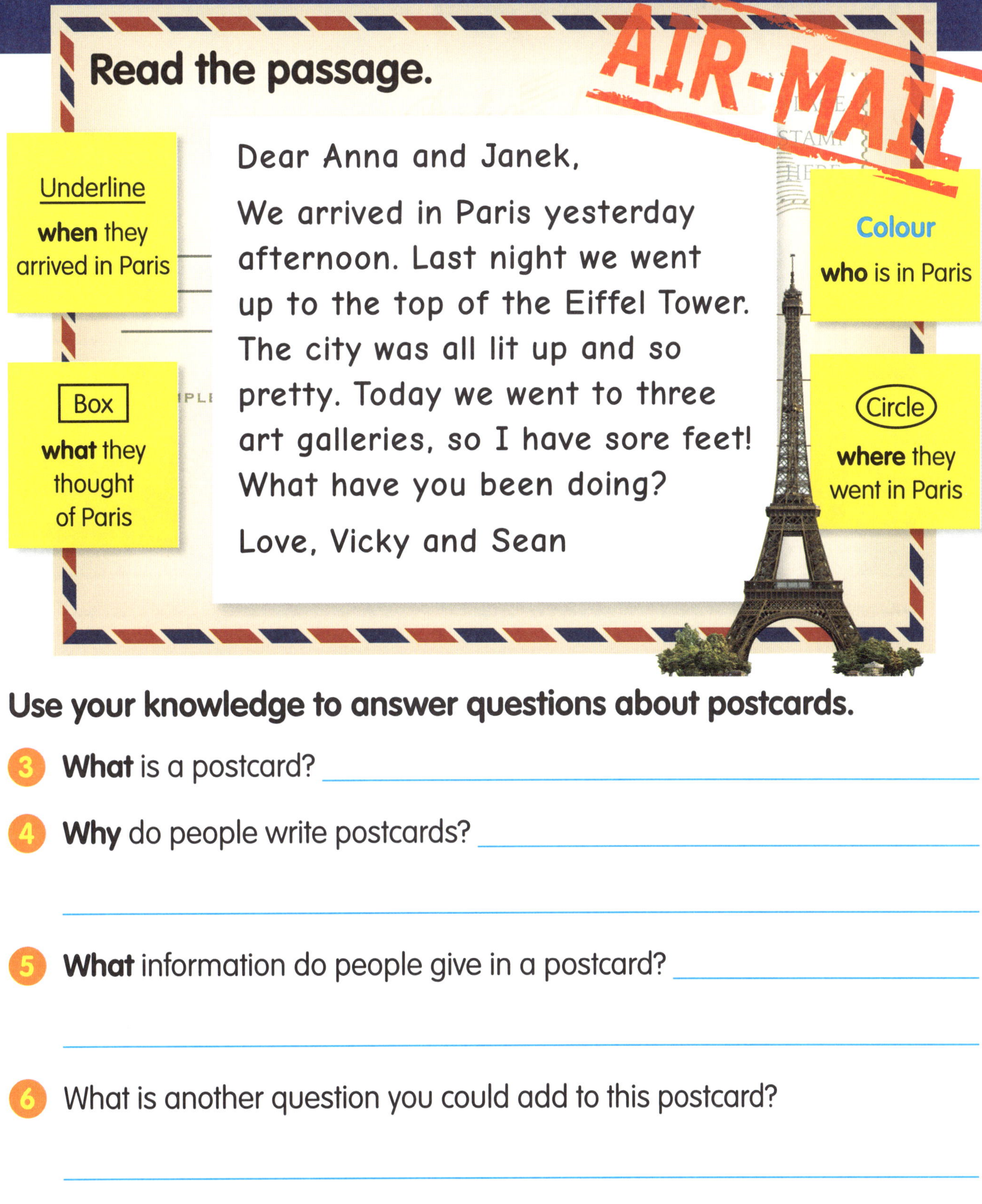


**Use your knowledge to answer questions about postcards.**

3 **What** is a postcard? ______________________________

4 **Why** do people write postcards? ______________________________

______________________________

5 **What** information do people give in a postcard? ______________________________

______________________________

6 What is another question you could add to this postcard?

______________________________

______________________________

______________________________

LESSON 40

# Signs

**Making Inferences**

Good readers use clues in the text and their own knowledge to work out word meanings. It helps to understand the author's intention.

## Sign 1

1 Use your **word knowledge** to complete these definitions.

**a** WILD + LIFE = WILDLIFE
Animals

**b** WATER + FOWL = WATERFOWL
A bird that

## Sign 2

2 Use your **word knowledge** to complete this paragraph.

The highest fire danger warning is ________________________. Another word which means the same is ________________________. People feel safest when the sign reads __________________.



**ACELY1670** Makes valid inferences using information in a text and students' own prior knowledge

**Think about the sign and answer the questions below.**

3 **What** does fragile mean? ______________________

4 Which **clue** helped you? ______________________

______________________

5 **Name** three things that are fragile. ______________________

______________________

6 **Where** would you expect to see this sign? ______________________

______________________

______________________

GRAMMAR LESSON 4

# Commas

**Commas (,)** are punctuation marks that separate words in lists. For example: **At the petting zoo I saw pigs, goats, lambs and rabbits**. The last two words are separated by the **conjunctions** *and* or *or*.

## Read the extract.

Highlight the **list** and circle the **commas**.

Colour the **list** and put a box around the **comma**.

Underline the **lists** and circle the **commas**.

### The Water Cycle

Water moves through a continuous cycle.

The sun heats water in oceans, rivers, lakes and creeks. The water turns into water vapour. This is called evaporation.

Water vapour rises and cools. It forms droplets that join together to make clouds. This is called condensation.

When the clouds get heavy, water falls from them as rain, hail or snow. This is called precipitation.

Water can be solid, liquid or gas. Examples are ice (solid), rain (liquid) and steam (gas).

The amount of water on Earth never changes. It's always moving through a part of the water cycle.

## After which word should there be a comma?

1. You can pour the water into a bottle jug or bucket.
   a water  b a  c bottle  d jug
2. People use water for drinking cleaning and growing food.
   a water  b drinking  c cleaning  d growing
3. Waste water comes from showers toilets and washing.
   a Waste  b from  c showers  d toilets
4. You should drink water before during and after playing sport.
   a drink  b before  c during  d after



**ACELA1465** Recognise that commas are used to separate items in lists

**5** **Fill in the commas in the following lists.**

a rain hail and snow

b trickle drip drizzle or pour

c wells tanks tubs and taps

d peaches pears grapes and watermelon

e watering can hosepipe spray bottle and sprinkler

**6** **Use the pictures to complete the sentence.**

You can pour the water into a ________________

________________________________

________________________________

**7** **In each sentence cross out the comma that isn't needed.**

a They get their water from springs, rivers, or streams.

b Swans, pelicans, gannets, and gulls are all water birds.

c At the beach you can swim, surf, build sandcastles, and sunbathe.

d You can see ducks, frogs, dragonflies, and mosquitoes around ponds.

e The children saw seaweed, limpets, sea stars, and sea urchins.

**8** **Complete each sentence with a list containing three items.**

a At the beach I ate ________________________________

____________________________________________

b My favourite drinks are ____________________________

____________________________________________

ASSESSMENT 2:

# Dolphins and Porpoises

There are 31 species of dolphin and six species of porpoise.

Some dolphin species, such as the bottlenose dolphin, live in oceans. Others live in coastal waters and rivers. Porpoises, such as the harbour porpoise, live in coastal waters.

Dolphins and porpoises eat fish and squid. They breathe through a blowhole, which closes when the animal is underwater. They have flippers and streamlined bodies. All dolphins and porpoises have a dorsal fin, except the finless porpoise.

Dolphins and porpoises mostly live and hunt in groups called pods. Pods protect dolphins from predators. If a shark attacks, bottlenose dolphins fiercely defend their pod. They ram the shark's soft belly with their snouts.

## Circle the correct answer.

1 How many species of dolphin are there? LITERAL

a thirty six
b thirty one
c thirteen
d thirty

2 Where do dolphins and porpoises live? LITERAL

a on land
b underground
c in water
d on the land and in water

3 What helps dolphins and porpoises swim fast? INFERENTIAL

a their flippers and streamlined bodies
b their blowholes
c their dorsal fins
d their bottle-shaped noses

4 Which statement is true? Dolphins and porpoises eat … LITERAL

a seaweed and seagrass.
b sharks and whales.
c small sea creatures.
d other dolphins and porpoises.

5 Where do dolphins and porpoises breathe? INFERENTIAL

a below the surface of the water
b above the surface of the water
c deep underwater
d on rocks and beaches

6 What is a group of dolphins called? LITERAL

a a herd
b a flock
c an army
d a pod

7 Which animals prey on dolphins and porpoises? LITERAL

a turtles
b seals
c sharks
d clown fish

8 Which word in the text shows that dolphins can be aggressive? VOCABULARY

a fiercely
b protect
c defend
d finless

9 In the text, which words can be used in place of *ram*? VOCABULARY

a push around
b squeeze hard
c pull apart
d crash into

10 Which part of the dolphin is its snout? INFERENTIAL

a the top of the head
b the mouth and nose
c the side of the head
d the tail

LESSON 41

# Artrageous

## Think Marks

To help us understand what we are reading, we can use **special marks**. These help us clearly see the parts we don't understand, and the connections we make to the text.

*I can see this part*

W

*What's this word?*

*I understand this part*

## Read the passage.

**Colour** **who** is in the story

**Circle** **what** Luke imagined

### Imagine This, Imagine That

"It's easy. One person starts imagining something that doesn't exist, say a flying car, and the next person has to add to it," said Luke.

"So you could imagine a flying car shaped like a fish," said Aunt Stella.

Sophie understood. "And the flying car shaped like a fish could spray fireworks from its wheels."

**Box** **what** Sophie imagined

**Underline** **what** Aunt Stella imagined

## Circle the correct answer.

1. **What** does Luke imagine?
   - a a flying car
   - b a fish in a flying car
   - c a flying car that can swim
   - d a fish spraying fireworks
2. **Who** is in the story?
   - a a fish, a flying car, Aunt Stella
   - b Aunt Stella, Luke, Sophie
   - c a fish named Fireworks, Aunt Sophie, a car
   - d Luke, a flying car, Spray
3. **Which** word could replace *understood* in this story?
   - a hugged
   - b won
   - c proved
   - d followed



**ACELY1670** Use comprehension strategies to build literal meaning

## Read the passage.
### Use Think Marks to help you understand the passage.

**what** Sophie collected

**adjectives** that describe what Sophie collected

**Colour** **what** Sophie liked best

### Art Eyes

"Look out for colours, patterns, shapes, textures and shadows that catch your attention. Draw them in your journal and collect as much treasure as you can!" Aunt Stella cried.

Sophie liked the shapes and colours of the shells. She collected lots of shells of all shapes, sizes, colours and patterns.

Sophie also rubbed some rock textures into her journal and drew a rough sketch of the beach. But her most precious find was a piece of blue, weathered glass.

4. **What** did Sophie collect? ______________________

5. **What** did Sophie draw? ______________________

6. **Which** word helps you understand that Sophie *valued* the piece of glass?

______________________

7. Write about a time you found something precious.

______________________

______________________

______________________

______________________

LESSON 42

# The World's Longest Toenail

## Making Inferences

To make inferences while reading, we have to use clues in the text.

The clues help us find the answers that are hiding in the text.

## Read the passage.

Circle **who** was trapped

Underline **what** trapped the person

Box **what** the people were doing

Colour **how** Jake felt

### Smelly and Stuck

Jake's toenail went PING! Jake spun around like a corkscrew. And there he stuck.

Everybody pushed and shoved. People with cameras took photos. People with notebooks asked questions.

"What does it feel like to be trapped by your toenail, Jake? they asked.

The sacks were full of fertiliser. The longest toenail in the world was no fun anymore.

## Circle the correct answer.

1. **Which** best describes how Jake was feeling?
   - a confused
   - b unhappy
   - c giddy
   - d happy

2. Which **clue** tells you this?
   - a Jake's toenail went PING!
   - b People pushed and shoved.
   - c "What does it feel like to be trapped by your toenail, Jake?"
   - d The sacks were full of fertiliser.
   - e The longest toenail in the world was no fun anymore.

3. What **inference** can we make about Jake?
   - a Jake is the centre of attention.
   - b Jake wants the longest toenail in the world.
   - c Jake wants to travel the world.
   - d Jake likes having his photo taken.

**ACELY1670** Makes valid inferences using information in a text and students' own prior knowledge

## Read the passage.

Circle **what** was growing

**Colour** **where** the toenail grew

### Sam's Cool Idea

The longest toenail in the world was growing.

Longer and wider and taller! And it was growing FAST!

It curled three times round his body. It shot past his ears. It twisted over his head. It snaked up past the diving board.

Jake gasped as his toenail snaked and grew. As big as himself ... as tall as a tree ... as big as a house ... as tall as a crane.

Underline the speed of Jake's growing toenail

4 **Draw** Jake and his enormous toenail.

5 How would you **feel** about having a very long toenail?

6 We can **infer** that Jake was worried. What is the clue?

LESSON 43

# A Hairy Question

**Visualisation**

Good readers imagine pictures when they read a text. This is called visualising. Looking for key words in the text helps us create the images.

## Read the passage.

Underline **what** Jan said about cooking

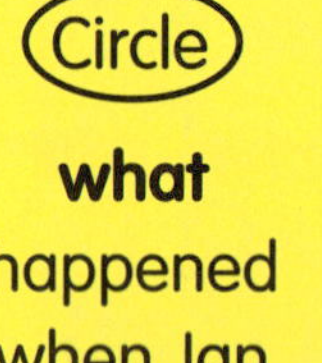

Circle **what** happened when Jan cooked

### The Home Haircut

"Easy," said Jan as she cut. "Piece of cake!"

I remember when Jan said cooking was easy. We spent an afternoon scraping burnt food off the stove.

Jan also told me that camping was easy. The tent fell on top of us during the night.

By three o'clock on Saturday afternoon there was more hair on the bathroom floor than on my head.

Box **what** Jan said about camping

Colour **what** happened when Jan camped

## Circle the correct answer.

1. Which **key word** describes **what** Jan thought about cooking?
   - a remember
   - b scraping
   - c easy
   - d more

2. Which phrase helps us **visualise** Jan's cooking?
   - a piece of cake
   - b cooking was easy
   - c scraping burnt food off the stove
   - d tent fell on top of us

3. How does this help the reader **see** Jan's cooking adventure? It was ...
   - a unsuccessful.
   - b lots of fun.
   - c a great success.
   - d tasteless.



**ACELY1670** Makes valid inferences using information in a text and students' own prior knowledge

## Read the passage.

**Circle** **what** Jan was doing

**Colour** words that **describe** Freya's new hairdo

**Underline** words that describe **how** Jan **felt**

### The Home Haircut

"Look in the mirror, Freya," said Jan.

I did. There was a lot of face and not much hair.

"Is it all right?" Jan said, looking worried.

"One side is longer than the other," I said softly.

Jan cut some more. Snip. Snip. Snip.

In the mirror, I looked strange. My hair was gone. Bits stuck out all over the place.

Jan's face was white.

4. What does **Freya think** of her new hairdo? ______________________

5. Which **clues** tell you? ______________________

______________________

6. Draw Freya and Jan's faces in the mirror.

**ACELY1670** Makes valid inferences using information in a text and students' own prior knowledge

LESSON 44

# Can I Join the Circus?

**Finding the Main Idea**

The main idea of a text is its key point. Details in the text can help us find the main idea.

This is a script. It is designed to be performed by different people.

## Read the passage.

**Colour** who is scared

**Underline** why he is scared

**Box** who is crying

**Ringmaster Roy:** Chuckles, perhaps you could teach Snoz about being a clown.

**Narrator:** Chuckles had a great time dressing Snoz and painting him with make-up. But when Snoz saw himself in the mirror, he hid under the table.

**Snoz:** Not funny! Too scary! Snoz is scared!

**Narrator:** Snoz began to cry. Seeing a Snozalot cry made Chuckles cry too.

**Chuckles:** (sobbing) That is the saddest thing I have ever seen. A sobbing Snozalot!

## Circle the correct answer/s.

1. Find the **main idea** of the text.
   - a Snoz is scared of himself as a clown.
   - b Chuckles is a clown.
   - c Clowns make people laugh.
   - d Snoz can't wait to join the circus.

2. Which two sentences **support** the main idea?
   - a Chuckles had a great time dressing Snoz and painting him with make-up.
   - b But when Snoz saw himself in the mirror, he hid under the table.
   - c Snoz began to cry.
   - d Seeing a Snozalot cry made Chuckles cry too.

## Read the passage.

the things Snoz **cannot** do

Underline

**what** Chuckles says about Snoz

**what** Bendy Betty says about Snoz

**what** Max Manyhands says about Snoz

**Ringmaster Roy:** Tell me troupe, what can Snoz the Snozalot Monster do?

**Chuckles:** I will tell you what he cannot do. He cannot make you laugh.

**Bendy Betty:** He cannot bend.

**Max Manyhands:** He cannot juggle.

**Ringmaster Roy:** I see, I see, I see. And I know he can't fly though the air.

**Chuckles:** He's a nice monster.

**Bendy Betty:** A lovely monster, really.

**Max Manyhands:** But Snoz has no place in Circus Bizurkus.

3 **Fill in the missing words.**

The main idea of the text is that ____________________ does not

belong in ________________________________.

4 Which **two details** helped you find the main idea?

a Everyone says Snoz can't ________________

________________________________

b Max Manyhands says Snoz has ________________

________________________________

LESSON 45

# The Lion and the Gnat

**Finding the Main Idea**

The main idea of a text is its key point. It sums up what the text is about.

Details in the text can help us find the main idea.

## Read the passage.

the gnat's **actions**

Underline the lion's **actions**

Box words that describe the lion's **feelings**

The gnat dived at the lion and stung him on the nose. The lion was furious! He swiped at the gnat, but only ended up scratching himself with his sharp claws. The gnat attacked the lion again and again, and the lion raged.

## Circle the correct answer/s.

1 Which **best** describes the main idea of the text?

a A lion attacked a gnat.
b A lion fell down.
c A gnat wanted to be a lion.
d A gnat attacked a lion.

2 Which **two** details **support** the main idea?

a The gnat dived at the lion and stung him on the nose.
b The lion was furious!
c He swiped at the gnat.
d The lion scratched himself with his sharp claws.
e The gnat attacked the lion again and again, and the lion raged.

3 Which **best** describes the gnat's actions?

a selfish
b kind
c gentle
d vicious



**ACELT1587** Discuss moral stories from varied cultures to identify and compare their central messages

## Read the passage.

Underline **what** the lion does

Finally, the lion was worn out. He was dripping with blood from his own scratches and he lay down, defeated by the gnat. The gnat buzzed away to tell the whole Animal Kingdom about his victory over the lion, but instead he flew straight into a spider's web.

Colour **what** the gnat does

4 What is the **main idea** of the text?

a The gnat celebrated a great victory.

b The smaller creature proved to be the more dangerous.

5 Which **two details** helped you find the main idea?

a *The lion was* ____________________________

________________________________________

b *The gnat had* ____________________________

________________________________________

6 What is the **message** from this fable? ____________________

________________________________________

GRAMMAR LESSON 5

# Compound Sentences

A **compound sentence** is when two simple sentences are joined to make a single sentence. They are joined with the **conjunctions** *or*, *and* or *but*. For example:

**Sam likes apples. His sister likes pears.**
**Sam likes apples and his sister likes pears.**
**Sam likes apples but his sister likes pears.**

## Read the extract.

Highlight the **compound sentence**. Circle the **conjunction**.

Colour the **compound sentence**. Put a box around the **conjunction**.

Underline the **compound sentence**. Circle the **conjunction**.

### Magic and Computers

Ellie knew about magic. She read stories about magic. In stories things happened and no one could explain why.

Gary never thought about magic, but he didn't read much. He was Ellie's brother and two years older.

When Ellie asked Gary if computers were magic, Gary laughed.

"Computers only do what they are programmed to do," said Gary.

"What does programmed mean?" Ellie asked.

Gary tried to explain. "A computer is built by people to work things out. People write programs and the computer follows the program's instructions."

## In each sentence, find the conjunction.

1. Ellie likes magic and her brother likes computers.
   a and  b likes  c her  d brother
2. Gary knew a lot about computers, but Ellie didn't.
   a lot  b about  c but  d didn't
3. Ellie can choose a book about magic or a book about computers.
   a can  b a  c about  d or
4. People write programs but they don't always work.
   a write  b but  c don't  d always



**ACELA1467** Understand that simple connections can be made between ideas by using a compound sentence with two or more clauses usually linked by a coordinating conjunction

**5** **Complete each sentence with *or, and* or *but.***

a He took out his computer ____________ switched it on.

b You can play a computer game ____________ you can watch TV.

c She has a computer ____________ she doesn't know how to use it.

d You can find information in a book ____________ you can search the Internet.

e I wanted to use the computer ____________ I couldn't remember the password.

**6** **Turn these sentences into compound sentences. Join them with *or, and* or *but.***

a Ellie likes to read. Gary likes to play computer games.

______________________________________________

______________________________________________

b You can use my tablet. You must look after it.

______________________________________________

______________________________________________

c Are you going to write the story? Are you going to type it?

______________________________________________

______________________________________________

**7** **Write endings for the following sentences.**

a Gary looked everywhere for his laptop but ______________________

______________________________________________

b Ellie sat at her desk and ______________________

______________________________________________

LESSON 46

# Dinosaur Dig

**Sequencing Events**

To find the sequence of events in a text, look at numbers and words that give clues to the order in which things happen.

## Read the passage.

**Circle** **where** you might find fossils

**Box** **what** the bones are removed from

### Finding Fossils

Places where rocks are eroding might have fossils. Creek banks, dry riverbeds and cliff faces are all good places to look. Most fossils are covered by a thick layer of rock. At some sites, explosives blow up the rock and bulldozers cart it away. Often the whole block of rock, with its bones, is cut out. This is taken back to the lab where the bones are carefully removed.

1. **Order** what happens when fossils are found

☐ Transport to a lab.

☐ Use explosives to blow up the rock.

☐ Find dinosaur bones.

☐ Use a bulldozer to remove the rock from the site.

☐ In the lab carefully remove the bones.

☐ Find a place with eroding rock—creek bank, riverbed or cliff face.

2. After this, **where** might children view the fossils? ______________________



**ACELY1670** Use comprehension strategies to build literal meaning

## Read the passage.

Underline the **first step** in putting a dinosaur back together

**what** happens after photos are taken and drawings made

**Colour** **how** the skeleton is put back together

### Giant Jigsaw Puzzles

Putting a dinosaur back together takes skill, patience and a lot of time.

Using photos and drawings, the skeleton is laid out on the floor and then put back together from the ground up.

Most bones are too fragile to become a skeleton in a museum. A plaster or plastic cast is made. It is rare to find a complete skeleton—most museums' dinosaurs are put together with extra parts.

3 **Draw** the process of putting together dinosaur skeletons.

| Step 1 | Step 2 |
|---|---|
| Step 3 | Step 4 |

LESSON 47

# Inventing the Future

## Finding Facts and Information

To find facts and information in a text, we usually ask the questions **Who? What? Where?** or **When?** The answers can be clearly seen in the text.

## Read the passage.

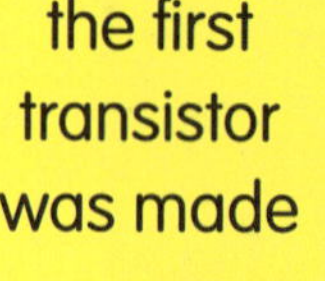

Circle **who** invented the transistor

Underline **when** the first transistor was made

Box **what** the first transistors were made from

Colour **where** transistors were first used

### A World-changing Gizmo

It all began in 1947. That's when three scientists invented the transistor. The three scientists were from the Bell Laboratories. Their names were John Bardeen, Walter Brattain and William Shockley.

The first transistor was about the size of your thumb. It was made from a paperclip, gold foil, wire and a bit of plastic. Transistors were first used in telephones.

Transistors are in computers, the Internet, mobile phones, TVs, video cameras, calculators, hand-held games, radar, satellites and night vision technology.

## Circle the correct answer.

1. **What** was the occupation of the inventors?

   a teachers b physiotherapists c scientists d professors

2. **What** size was the first transistor?

   a paperclip-sized b thumb-sized
   c mobile phone-sized d telephone-sized

3. **Where** are transistors used today?

   a paperclips b mobile phones c plastic d your thumb



**ACELY1670** Use comprehension strategies to build literal meaning

## Read the passage.

**Highlight** **what** Dr Nakamatsu holds the world record for

**Underline** **what** Dr Nakamatsu invented

**Box** **when** Dr Nakamatsu likes inventing

**Colour** **where** Dr Nakamatsu invents

### Why Didn't I Think of That?

Dr Nakamatsu is a modern inventor. He holds the world record for the most patents and inventions. Dr Nakamatsu has over 3200 inventions.

Dr Nakamatsu often came up with ideas underwater. He invented a notepad that he could use underwater to write down his ideas.

Dr Nakamatsu only sleeps four hours a night. He says the best time for new ideas is between midnight and 4 am. He has two special rooms that help him think.

4. **What** was Dr Nakamatsu's underwater problem?

5. **What** was Dr Nakamatsu's solution?

6. Think of a problem that you could invent a gizmo for.

| **Who** would need it? | **What** would it be? | **Where** would it be used? | **When** would it be needed? |
|---|---|---|---|
| | | | |

LESSON 48

# Boats

**Compare and Contrast**

When we compare and contrast information, we look for the similarities and differences.

## Read the passage.

### Moving People

People travel short distances on ferries. Cruise ships can take you all the way around the world.

Ferries travel across rivers, harbours and lakes. Some people catch ferries to work or school. Larger ferries also travel between islands or even between countries.

People take holidays on cruise ships. You live on the ship as it travels to different cities and countries. Cruise ships have restaurants, shops, movie theatres and bedrooms called cabins.

1 Compare and contrast everyday boats we use. [✔] the correct answers on the table.

| | Travels on and between | | | | | Travel for | | | Time spent on board | | On board | | |
|---|---|---|---|---|---|---|---|---|---|---|---|---|---|
| | rivers | harbours | lakes | cities | countries | work | holiday | school | Minutes or hours | Days or weeks | shops | movie theatres | restrooms |
| ferry | | | | | | | | | | | | | |
| cruise ship | | | | | | | | | | | | | |

**Use the information in the table to answer the questions below.**

2 What would you find on **both** ferries and cruise ships?

_______________________________________________

3 Between which two places do both ferries and cruise ships travel?

_______________________________________________



**ACELY1670** Use comprehension strategies to build inferred meaning

## Read the passage.

### The Navy

Destroyers, submarines and aircraft carriers are all used by the navy.

Destroyers are fast. They are often used to protect bigger, slower ships. They can hold up to 300 people.

Submarines travel under the water. They hold up to 150 people and can move quickly if they must.

Aircraft carriers are the biggest ships in the navy. They carry planes which can take off and land on their long decks. They can have up to 5000 sailors and pilots on board at any one time.

4 Complete the table.

| Boat | What does it do? | How many people can it hold? | Interesting fact |
|---|---|---|---|
| destroyer | | | |
| submarine | | | |
| aircraft carriers | | | |

5 **How** are destroyers, submarines and aircraft carriers similar?

LESSON 49

# Invitations

**Visualisation**

Good readers imagine pictures when they read a text. This is called visualising. Looking for key words in the text helps us create images.

## Read the passage.

Circle **who** is having the party

Underline **who** is invited to the party

To: Kosoko

From: Matilda

Please come to my: 8th birthday party

Where: Memorial Park, Dale Street

When: Saturday, 14 September

RSVP: 0499 853 627

Box **what** the party is for

Colour **when** the party will be held

## Circle the correct answer.

1. **Who** is having an 8th birthday party?

   a Matilda  b Kosoko  c Dale  d Parker

2. **Which** month is the party?

   a August  b November  c February  d September

3. **Which** street is Memorial Park on?

   a Kosoko St  b Dale St  c Saturday St  d Park St

4. Write down games you have played at a birthday party.



ACELY1670 Makes valid inferences using information in a text and students' own prior knowledge

# Read the passage.

Circle **who** is having the sleepover

Underline **who** is invited to the sleepover

Box **what** they will eat

Colour **what** they will play

Dear Amy,

I am going to have a sleepover at my house next Friday. Do you want to come? We will play games, eat lots of pizza and stay up really late. Mum says that she can drive you home the next morning. My address is 48 Trig Street. Please let me know if your mum and dad say it is OK to come. It will be lots of fun!

Bye,
Hua

5 Draw pictures of the images you create in your head of the sleepover. Make connections to sleepovers you have been to and add extra information.

| What will you see? | What will you taste? | What will you smell? | What will you hear? |
|---|---|---|---|
| | | | |

LESSON 50

# Mammals

**Making Inferences**

Good readers know how to study words in the context of the text. We can often use clues in the text to help us work out the meaning of words we do not understand.

## Read the passage.

### Hoofed Mammals

*Hoofed mammals eat plants. They are herbivores. Zebras, giraffes and elephants are all hoofed mammals.*

Many hoofed mammals live in groups called herds. They often live on open plains or grasslands. The herd moves from place to place in search of food. Zebras and wildebeests live in large herds.

Elephants are the largest land animals. They live in family groups called herds. Baby elephants feed on mother's milk for two years while they grow.

Circle the **hoofed animals**

Underline the **collective noun**

Box **two verbs** that tell what baby elephants do

## Circle the correct answer.

1 Which **best** describes how hoofed animals live?

a in harmony with many other animals

b on their own

c in pairs

d in large groups

2 Which **clue** tells you this?

a Hoofed mammals eat plants.

b Zebras, giraffes and elephants are all hoofed mammals.

c Many hoofed mammals live in groups called herds.

d The herd moves from place to place in search of food.

e Elephants are the largest land animals.



ACELY1670 Makes valid inferences using information in a text and students' own prior knowledge

## Read the passage.

Underline the word that **compares** the **size** of apes and monkeys

Box the word that **compares** the **size** of gorillas and other apes

### Monkeys and Apes

*Monkeys and apes are mammals called primates. They are warm-blooded, furry animals that suckle their young.*

Baboons, mandrills and howlers are all monkeys. Monkeys are very good climbers. They use their hands, feet and tails to help them climb.

Apes are larger than monkeys. Chimpanzees, gibbons, orangutans and gorillas are all apes. Apes do not have tails.

Gorillas are the largest of all the apes and are tailless. They live in family groups.

**Colour which** primates have tails

**which** primates don't have tails

3 Use the information to order the size of primates.

| small | larger | largest |
|---|---|---|
| | | |

4 What is the physical difference between monkeys and apes?

______________________________

5 Which **clue** tells you? ______________________________

______________________________

# Time Connectives

**Connectives** link words or ideas in a text. **Time connectives** are **words** or **phrases** that tell **when** something happens.

For example: **first, then, next, eventually, this morning, a little while later.**

## Read the extract.

**Highlight when** Bertram was born.

**Colour when** Beatrix became interested in studying fungi.

**Circle when** Beatrix published her first book.

Put a box around **when** a company agreed to publish Beatrix's book.

### Beatrix Potter

Beatrix Potter is famous for writing children's books. Her best-known book is *The Tale of Peter Rabbit.*

Beatrix was born in England in 1866. Six years later, her brother Bertram was born.

As children, Beatrix and Bertram enjoyed sketching. Beatrix spent hours copying art from books and artworks.

In her twenties, Beatrix became very interested in studying fungi. She even wrote a paper on them. But scientists did not value her work because she was a woman.

After that, Beatrix began to focus on her art. She also started writing stories. In 1901 she published *The Tale of Peter Rabbit* herself for her family and friends. A year later, a company agreed to publish it. It was a huge success.

## In each sentence, find the time connective.

1 A publishing company eventually agreed to publish *The Tale of Peter Rabbit.*

a A publishing company b eventually c agreed d to publish

2 A company finally agreed to publish Beatrix's book.

a finally b agreed c A company d to publish

3 In the 1800s, it was hard for women to have a career.

a In b 1800s c In the 1800s d was hard



**ACELA1464** Understand how texts are made cohesive through language features, including word associations

4 **In each sentence, circle the correct word in brackets.**

a I read *The Tale of Peter Rabbit* (before, afterwards) *The Tale of Tom Kitten.*

b (While, Next) I'm going to read *The Story of Miss Moppet.*

c *The Tale of Mrs Tittlemouse* was written (eventually, after) *The Tale of the Flopsy Bunnies.*

d I am going to read *The Tale of Benjamin Bunny* (tonight, yesterday).

e I have (lastly, finally) found a copy of *The Tale of Squirrel Nutkin.*

5 **Complete each of the following sentences.**

a This morning ______________________________

______________________________

b Next week ______________________________

______________________________

6 **Fill in the gaps with connectives from the box.**

Beatrix Potter **A** first started sketching when she was a child. **B** ______________ she became interested in fungi. **C** ______________ her work on fungi was not taken seriously, she began to focus on her art. **D** ______________ she wrote and illustrated children's books. **E** ______________ her books are still popular around the world.

| Eventually | Later | Today | ~~first~~ | After |
|---|---|---|---|---|

ASSESSMENT 3:

# Ming Ming's Adventure

Ming Ming lived in the village of Jizhou. She was a daydreamer. She liked to pretend she was a princess.

Her father complained that she was a lazy child, but her mother said she had a good heart.

One day, Ming Ming's mother sent Ming Ming into the mountains to collect herbs. Her mother warned her to concentrate because the paths were dangerous.

Ming Ming set off. Before long, she was lost in her own imaginary world and tripped over a fallen log. She fell and smashed the special basket her mother had given her.

"Oh no!" she cried. "How will I carry the herbs home? Mother will never forgive me."

As Ming Ming wiped away her tears, she noticed some hollow seed pods nearby. She would use those to carry the herbs she collected.

When Ming Ming returned to the village, she told her parents what had happened. Her father praised his daughter for clever thinking.

## Circle the correct answer.

1 Which country is the village of Jizhou likely to be in? INFERENTIAL

a Australia  b America  c England  d China

2 We can infer that Ming Ming didn't always do her chores. Which phrase is the clue? INFERENTIAL

a a good heart  b a lazy child  c a quiet spot  d a young girl

3 Why did Ming Ming go into the mountains? LITERAL

a to pick flowers
b to collect herbs
c to sit and daydream
d to look for seed pods

4 Which words best describe Ming Ming? CRITICAL

a lazy and cruel
b kind and imaginative
c hardworking and clever
d clumsy and sad

5 Which word is closest in meaning to *concentrate*? VOCABULARY

a listen
b watch
c focus
d manage

6 What happened first? LITERAL

a Ming Ming collected the herbs.
b The basket broke.
c Ming Ming tripped.
d Ming Ming saw the seed pods.

7 Why was Ming Ming crying? She … INFERENTIAL

a was upset about the broken basket.
b hurt herself when she tripped.
c was scared of her father.
d couldn't find any herbs.

8 What is the main purpose of the text? CRITICAL

a to give information
b to tell a story
c to explain how something works
d to state a point of view

9 What is the main message of the text? LITERAL

a Respect your parents.
b Take care of other people's things.
c Every problem has a solution.
d Look where you're going.

10 Why did Ming Ming's father praise his daughter? For her … LITERAL

a honesty
b cleverness
c bravery
d hard work

LESSON 51

# Zac's Story

### Making Inferences

To make inferences we use clues in the text. The clues help us find the answers that are hiding in the text. This text is told from Danny's point of view.

## Read the passage.

Circle **who** was asked to read

Box **who** played computer games

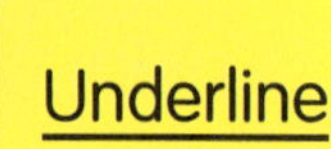
Underline the **excuse** for not reading

### Zac the Champion

Mr McFee asked Zac to read aloud. Zac said he couldn't find his glasses. He said his mother would look for them after work.

"Can't you see without your glasses?" I asked.

Zac shook his head.

After school, Zac came to my place. We played computer games on my Dad's computer.

Zac could see well enough to play them. He won every game.

## Circle the correct answer.

1. **What** was Zac unable to find?
   - a his computer
   - b his mother
   - c his glasses
   - d his work

2. **Why** did Danny think it was strange that Zac won the computer games?
   - a Zac played without his glasses.
   - b Zac hadn't won a game before.
   - c Zac played with his eyes closed.
   - d Zac said he didn't like to play.

3. What **inference** can you make about Danny?
   - a Danny is competitive and wanted to win the game.
   - b Danny thinks Zac is lying about needing glasses.
   - c Danny is an excellent reader but not a good computer game player.
   - d Danny and Zac are going to be good friends forever.



**ACELY1670** Makes valid inferences using information in a text and students' own prior knowledge

## Read the passage.

**who** visited Zac

**Colour** **what** Zac was doing when Nina and Danny arrived

### Zac Skips School

The next day Zac didn't come to school. Nina and Danny went to Zac's house after school. He was watching a cartoon.

When he saw them he rolled around on the floor. He held his stomach.

"I have a very bad migraine," he said. "Mum's going to take me to the doctor."

Underline **what** Zac said was wrong

Box **which** part of his body Zac held

4 **How** was Zac feeling?

5 Which **clues** tell you?

6 Is Zac lying? What is the clue?

7 **Why** might Zac be lying about being sick?

LESSON 52

# Computer Virus

### Drawing Conclusions

To draw conclusions from a text, we have to use clues to make our own judgments.

The clues help us find the answers that are hiding in the text.

## Read the passage.

Circle three verbs that show **how Vinnie moved**

Underline Vinnie's **dialogue**

Box a word that shows **how Vinnie's mum felt**

Colour Mum's **dialogue**

### The Sniffles

Vinnie raced in the front door. His bag skidded across the living room floor.

"What's going on in here?" Vinnie's mum stood in the doorway, hands on her hips.

Vinnie walked over and picked up his bag.

"Sorry, Mum. I'm in a bit of a hurry."

"What about a snack?"

"I'm not hungry."

Mary stood in shock as she watched him run up the stairs.

## Circle the correct answer.

1. Which is the best **conclusion**?
   - a Vinnie was in a rush.
   - b Vinnie likes doing his homework.
   - c Vinnie is hungry.
   - d Vinnie likes to keep things neat and tidy.

2. Which two words are **clues** to question 1's answer?
   - a walked
   - b raced
   - c run
   - d stood

3. Which is the best **conclusion**?
   - a Mum is untidy and doesn't like tidying.
   - b Mum doesn't like making snacks.
   - c Mum was surprised Vinny didn't want a snack.
   - d Vinnie was tired from a long day at school.

## Read the passage.

**Colour** words that describe **Dr. Hacker's arrival**

Box Dr. Hacker's **dialogue**

### Dr Hacker

Vinnie pulled the ad from his pocket and dialled the number.

"Hello," said the voice on the other end of the line.

"Are you Dr. Hacker?" asked Vinnie.

"That's right."

Vinnie explained his problem.

"Never fear, young Vinnie. I'll be there in a flash," said Dr. Hacker.

Vinnie hung up. Smoke filled the hall and a flash of light blinded him.

Dr. Hacker waved away the smoke. "Show me your sick computer."

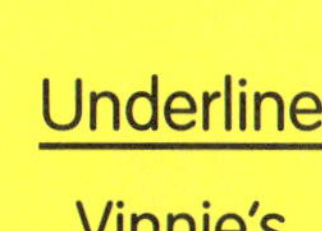

Underline Vinnie's **dialogue**

4. What can we **conclude** about Vinnie's problem?

5. From his arrival, what can we **conclude** about Dr. Hacker?

6. Which **clues** tell you?

*The text says, "*

LESSON 53

# Game Plan

**Making Predictions**

We can predict what is going to happen in a text based on clues in the words and pictures and what we already know.

## Read the passage.

Dear Sophie,

Thanks for your letter. I am sending you and your friend Luke my latest Cosmic Creature called Radiant. I would be delighted to share a few tricks of the trade with you and Luke. I will send my helicopter to pick you up at 10:15am this Saturday, from the soccer field near your house. Bring Gizmo along too.

Don't be late. I don't like to wait.

Yours in fun,
Professor Flukelar

## Circle the correct answers.

1. Which two **predictions** can you make about what will happen next in the story?
   - a Luke will forget to bring Gizmo, and Professor Flukelar will be angry.
   - b Sophie and Luke will spend the day with Professor Flukelar.
   - c Sophie will break her Cosmic Creature because she doesn't like it.
   - d Sophie and Luke will learn many new ideas from Professor Flukelar.

2. What **evidence** is there in the text to support your predictions?
   - a Don't be late.
   - b I am sending you and your friend Luke my latest Cosmic Creature called Radiant.
   - c I would be delighted to share a few tricks of the trade with you and Luke.
   - d Thanks for your letter.
   - e Bring Gizmo along too.



**ACELY1670** Use comprehension strategies to build inferred meaning

## Read the passage.

**'What if ...'**

"But how do you think of things like that?" asked Sophie.

"Yeah," said Luke. "How do you get to be the one who sees something in a new way, when no one else has?"

"Well," said the professor smiling, "there are a few little tricks that I can share with you."

The professor led them into his workroom. It was lined with his wonderful creations. All the Cosmic Creatures were there, as well as his siren balls, superfast glider kits and stretchable blocks.

3 **What** prediction can you make about what Sophie and Luke will learn from Professor Flukelar?

4 Predict **one** piece of advice the professor will give Sophie and Luke.

5 Draw what a Cosmic Creature might look like.

LESSON 54

# Haikus

## Visualisation

Good readers imagine pictures when they read. They use their senses to help them visualise. Haiku poems show a moment in time. They have few words and readers fill in the gaps by visualising.

## Read the passage.

Circle the **things** in the room

Box the **punctuation marks**

A man, just one—
also a fly, just one—
in the huge drawing room

**Kobayashi Issa**

Underline the **adjectives**

Colour the **repeated** phrase

## Circle the correct answers.

1. Which **two** things are in the drawing room?

   a man b huge c bay d fly

2. Which **two** punctuation marks are used?

   a question marks b commas
   c colons d dashes

3. **What** do these punctuation marks tell the reader to do?

   a shout b pause c whisper d look up

4. Which word **best** describes how the drawing room would look?

   a crowded b empty c full d noisy



**ACELY1670** Makes valid inferences using information in a text and students' own prior knowledge

## Read the passage.

Circle the **sound** words

Box the word that describes the **feel** of the egg

Warm snug speckled egg
Dappled light fading quickly
Soft crack of split shell

Alysha Hodge

Underline the word that describes what the egg **looks like**

**Colour** words that describe the **light**

## Circle the correct answer.

5 At what **time of day** is the poet looking at the egg?

a morning b late at night c midday d late afternoon

6 Which phrase describes the **sound** of the egg breaking?

a dappled b warm snug c fading quickly d soft crack

7 To hear this sound, how far away is the poet from the egg?

a far away
b behind it in a field
c very close
d in the next town

8 What is the poet **seeing**?

a a person taking a photo of an egg
b two chickens wrapped in a warm blanket
c two farmers ploughing the field
d a bird hatching

**ACELY1670** Makes valid inferences using information in a text and students' own prior knowledge

LESSON 55

# The Fox and the Grapes

### Finding the Main Idea

The main idea of a text is its key point. It sums up what the text is about. Details in the text can help us find the main idea.

## Read the passage.

Circle words that describe the **fox**

**Colour** the fox's **dialogue**

Underline words that describe the **grapes**

A hungry fox was looking for food. She saw bunches of juicy, plump grapes growing high up on a farmer's fence.

"I will have those grapes. I'm starving!" she said.

## Circle the correct answers.

1. Which **best** describes the main idea of the text?
   - a A fox wanted to become a farmer.
   - b A farmer was growing juicy, plump grapes.
   - c A greedy farmer put food too high for the fox.
   - d A hungry fox was looking for food.

2. Which **two** phrases **support** the main idea?
   - a growing high up
   - b hungry fox
   - c plump grapes
   - d I'm starving!

3. Which **best** describes what the fox plans to do?
   - a Steal the fence.
   - b Eat the grapes.
   - c Starve the farmer.
   - d Grow grapes.



**ACELT1587** Discuss moral stories from varied cultures to identify and compare their central messages

## Read the passage.

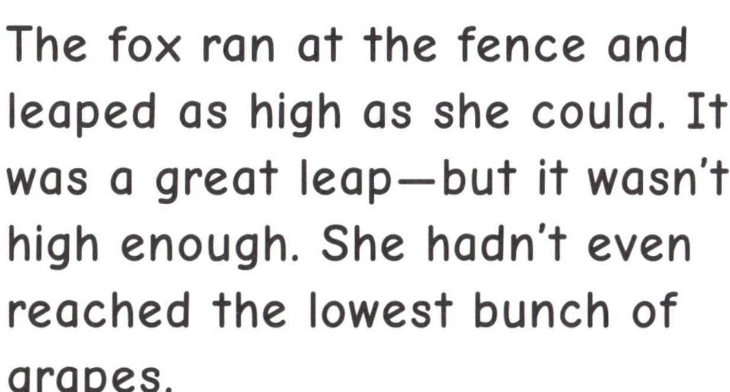

The fox ran at the fence and leaped as high as she could. It was a great leap—but it wasn't high enough. She hadn't even reached the lowest bunch of grapes.

The fox tried again. She ran and leaped and it was another wonderful leap. But once again, she did not jump high enough to reach the fruit. She didn't give up though.

Circle **two verbs** that tell how the fox moved

Underline **adjectives** that describe the leaps

Box **what** the fox was trying to reach

4 What is the **main idea**?

a The fox wanted the grapes.

b The fox tried unsuccessfully to reach the grapes.

c The fox refused to give up.

5 Which **two details** helped you find the main idea?

a The fox leaped

b The fox tried

GRAMMAR LESSON 7

# Action Verbs

An **action verb** tells what action is happening. For example: **The boys <u>run</u> home. The girls <u>ran</u> home.** Some verbs, like **think, feel** and **imagine,** show what is happening in our heads.

## Read the extract.

Circle the **verb** that means the same as *got to*.

Put a box around the **verb** that tells what the hens did.

Highlight the **verb** that tells how Violet gets up high.

Colour two **verbs** in the last sentence.

### Has Anyone Seen My Chook?

Hazel followed the seawall past the flooded houses until she reached the coconut grove.

Nearby, perched on the branch of a dead mango tree, was Loki, the chicken boy. Beside him sat his six fat hens.

"Have you seen my chook, Violet?" Hazel asked Loki.

"No, I haven't seen her. Maybe the waves got her. Maybe a big fish got her."

Hazel shook her head. "Violet always flies up high when the tide comes in. Are you taking your hens to school today?"

"No, there are too many. I am taking this." Loki reached into his shirt pocket and pulled out a tiny, chirping chick.

## In each sentence, find the action verb.

1. Hazel looked all over for her chook.
   - a over
   - b for
   - c looked
   - d chook
2. Loki perched on the branch of a dead mango tree.
   - a perched
   - b branch
   - c dead
   - d mango
3. Hazel shook her head.
   - a Hazel
   - b shook
   - c her
   - d head
4. Loki sometimes took his hens to school.
   - a sometimes
   - b school
   - c hens
   - d took



**ACELA1462** Identify language that can be used for appreciating texts and the qualities of people and things

**5 Complete each sentence with a verb from the box.**

a Hazel ________________ baked breadfruit and fish for breakfast.

b Hazel ________________ her chook Violet.

c Hazel's brothers ________________ a sandbag wall around their house.

d Violet and Loki ________________ to school every day.

e Violet ________________ through the water under her house.

f Hazel's father ________________ fruit in Australia.

| walk | eats | built | picks | named | waded |
|---|---|---|---|---|---|

**6 Colour the verbs that tell what a bird can do.**

**7 Complete each sentence by filling in a verb.**

a Our hens ________________ eggs every day.

b Hazel ________________ her chook in the hen house.

LESSON 56

# Wet

**Visualisation**

Good readers imagine pictures when they read a text. This is called visualising. Looking for key words in the text helps us create the images.

## Read the passage.

**Colour** **where** tigers live

**Box** a word that **describes** a tiger's coat

**Underline** **why** a tiger's prey doesn't hear it coming

### Bengal Tigers

*Some Bengal tigers live in the mangrove forests of India and Bangladesh.*

Tigers hunt mammals, such as wild boars. Bengal tigers also eat saltwater crabs and fish.

Tigers are quick and powerful hunters. They have soft foot pads that help them quietly stalk prey. Their striped coats help tigers hide in the forest. Every tiger has a different pattern of stripes.

## Circle the correct answers.

1. **Where** do Bengal tigers live?

   a at the park   b in the snow   c by the ocean   d in the forest

2. **Why** might tigers be difficult to spot?

   a Tigers' stripes help camouflage them.
   b Tigers hunt at night and sleep all day.
   c Tigers have excellent eyesight.
   d Tigers have soft foot pads.

3. Draw three things tigers eat.



**ACELY1670** Makes valid inferences using information in a text and students' own prior knowledge

## Read the passage.

Colour **where** hippos live

Box **how** a hippo moves

Underline **what** is on top of a hippo's head

### Hippopotamuses

*Hippos live in swampy lakes and rivers in Africa.*

Hippos spend the day in the water. A hippo's eyes, ears and nostrils are on the top of its head. It can watch for danger while the rest of its body is underwater.

Hippos nurse their young and even sleep underwater. Hippos do not truly swim. They run or walk along the river bed.

Hippos are often aggressive. They open their mouths to warn off intruders.

4. Draw and label a picture of a hippo based on information in this text. You can make connections to hippos you've read about in stories, seen on safari or at the zoo.

LESSON 57

# Farms

**Compare and Contrast**

When we compare and contrast information, we look for similarities and differences.

## Read the passage.

### Vegetables

Many vegetables need a certain temperature to grow well. Some vegetables that grow well in cooler weather are carrots, onions and winter lettuce. Tomatoes, corn and capsicums need hot, sunny weather to grow well.

Some vegetables, such as lettuce and capsicums, are quick growing. Lettuce is ready to eat in six to eight weeks. Other vegetables, such as carrots, tomatoes, onions and corn take four to five months to grow and ripen.

1 Complete the table using ticks [✔].

| Vegetable | Grows best in cooler weather | Grows best in warmer weather | Quick to grow | Longer to grow |
|---|---|---|---|---|
| carrot | | | | |
| corn | | | | |
| capsicum | | | | |
| onion | | | | |
| winter lettuce | | | | |
| tomato | | | | |

2 Put a [✔] next to true information.

a ☐ Carrots and corn are quick-growing vegetables.

b ☐ Onions and tomatoes are best to grow in winter.

c ☐ Capsicums are quick-growing vegetables that like warm weather.

d ☐ You would have more tomatoes and corn in summer than in winter.

e ☐ Winter lettuce likes cool weather.



**ACELY1670** Use comprehension strategies to build inferred meaning

## Read the passage.

Box **what** farmers use **cows** for

Underline the name for a **group of cows**

### Cows and Sheep

*Some farmers raise large herds of cattle. Others raise large flocks of sheep.*

Farmers raise herds of cows, called cattle, for their meat and hides. Leather is made into shoes, clothes and furniture. Cattle eat grass in fields or are fed hay and grain.

Dairy cows make milk. Milk can be made into cheese, yogurt and ice cream.

Farmers raise sheep for their wool, meat and milk. Farmers shear sheep once a year. The wool can be made into sweaters, blankets and carpets.

Colour **what** farmers use **sheep** for

Circle the name for a **group of sheep**

3 Use the information in the text to compare and contrast sheep and cattle.

**Compare and contrast products we get from sheep and cattle.**

Sheep

Sheep and Cattle

Cattle

LESSON 58

# Fighter Planes

**Sequencing Events**
To identify the sequence of events in a text, look at words that give clues to the order in which things happen.

## Read the passage.

Box
**what** gets a plane off the ground

### How a jet engine works

Jet engines burn a mixture of fuel and air. This makes hot gases, which give thrust. Thrust gets a plane off the ground and keeps it moving.

Underline
**how** hot gases are made

1. What does a jet engine burn?

   a thrust and ground
   b fuel and air
   c gases and thrust
   d jets and air

2. Order the events using the numbers 1–5.

   ☐ The hot gases give thrust.
   ☐ Thrust lifts a plane off the ground
   ☐ Jet engines burn a mixture of fuel and air.
   ☐ Thrust keeps the fighter plane moving.
   ☐ The mix of fuel and air makes hot gases.



ACELY1670 Use comprehension strategies to build literal meaning

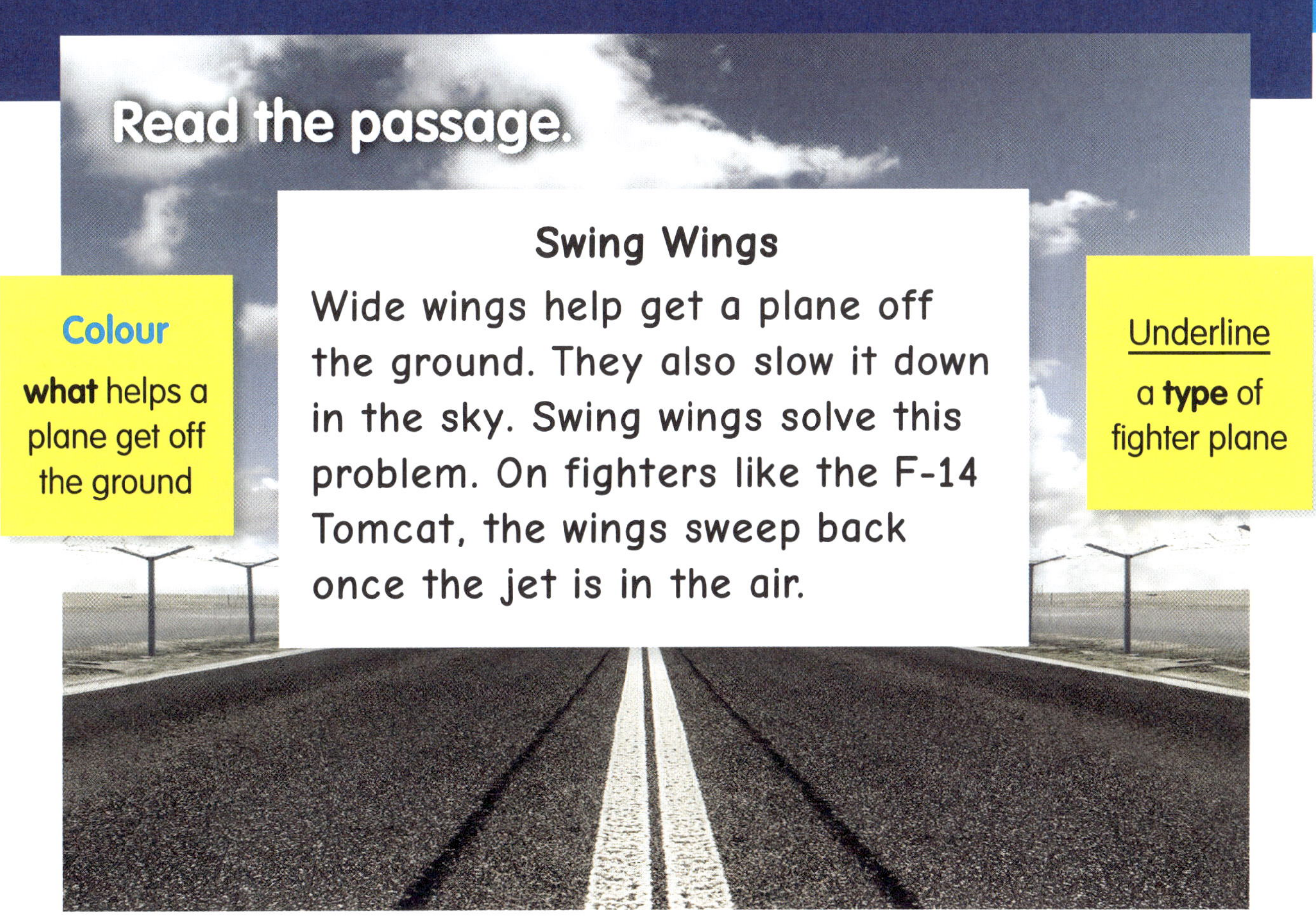


**Colour** **what** helps a plane get off the ground

## Swing Wings

Wide wings help get a plane off the ground. They also slow it down in the sky. Swing wings solve this problem. On fighters like the F-14 Tomcat, the wings sweep back once the jet is in the air.

Underline a **type** of fighter plane

3 **What** helps a plane take off?

4 On an F-14 Tomcat, **where** are the wings at take-off?

5 On an F-14 Tomcat, **when** do the wings sweep back?

6 **What** do you predict will happen to the wings when it is time to land?

LESSON 59

# Healthy Foods

**Compare and Contrast**

When we compare and contrast information, we look for the similarities and differences between details in the text.

## Read the passage.

Underline **what** is in a balanced diet

Circle different **types** of food

Colour **why** we need good food

### Healthy Foods

*Your body needs a variety of good foods to grow and stay healthy.*

The food we eat is called our diet. A balanced diet contains a wide variety of foods.

Carbohydrates in foods such as bread and rice give us energy. Other foods, like fruits and vegetables, are full of vitamins and minerals.

We need protein to make muscles, skin and hair. Meat and eggs are high-protein foods. We need calcium for our teeth and bones. Dairy foods, like cheese and milk, are high in calcium.

1 Complete the table.

| | Why we need them | Examples |
|---|---|---|
| Carbohydrates | | |
| Fruit and vegetables | | |
| Protein | | |
| Dairy | | |



ACELY1670 Use comprehension strategies to build inferred meaning

## Read the passage.

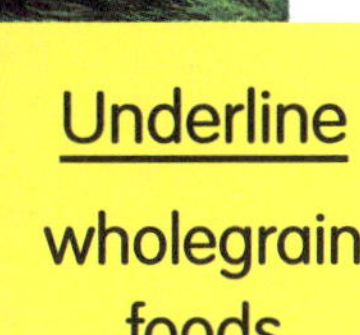

Box what can be made with grains

Circle what grains give the body

Underline wholegrain foods

### Grains

A healthy diet should include grains, such as wheat, rice and corn.

Some grain is cooked and eaten whole. These are wholegrain foods. Other grain is ground into flour to make bread, pasta and cereals. All grains have carbohydrates, which give the body energy.

Some wholegrain foods are corn on the cob, rice and wholegrain bread. They are high in fibre. Wholegrains contain magnesium, a mineral that helps build strong bones and teeth.

2. What do all grains give the body?

3. What extra nutrients do wholegrains give the body?

4. What is magnesium good for?

LESSON 60

# Clothes

**Making Inferences**

To make inferences we use clues in the text. The clues help us find the answers that are hiding in the text.

## Read the passage.

Circle **when** machinery for making clothes was invented

Box **the adjective** that describes clothes of the 1800s

Underline **the invention** that led to clothes being mass-produced

### 1800s

*During the 1800s, machinery for making clothes was invented. More factories were built. Textiles became mass-produced.*

Before machinery, weavers and tailors made clothes by hand.

Sewing machines were invented and then mass-produced during the 1800s. This allowed women at home to make clothing quickly and easily. Clothes of the 1800s were often uncomfortable to wear. Women wore bone corsets that laced up tightly.

## Circle the correct answer.

1. Which **best** describes the big change in the clothing industry in the 1800s?
   - a Machinery was used to make clothes.
   - b Sewing machines were affordable but uncomfortable.
   - c Women liked to make fashionable clothing.
   - d Men made clothes.

2. Which **clues** tell you this?
   - a Women wore bone corsets that laced up tightly.
   - b During the 1800s, machinery for making clothes was invented.
   - c More factories were built.
   - d Clothes of the 1800s were often uncomfortable to wear.
   - e Sewing machines were invented and then mass-produced during the 1800s.
   - f This allowed women at home to make clothing quickly and easily.



**ACELY1670** Makes valid inferences using information in a text and students' own prior knowledge

## Read the passage.

Underline popular clothes in the 1990s

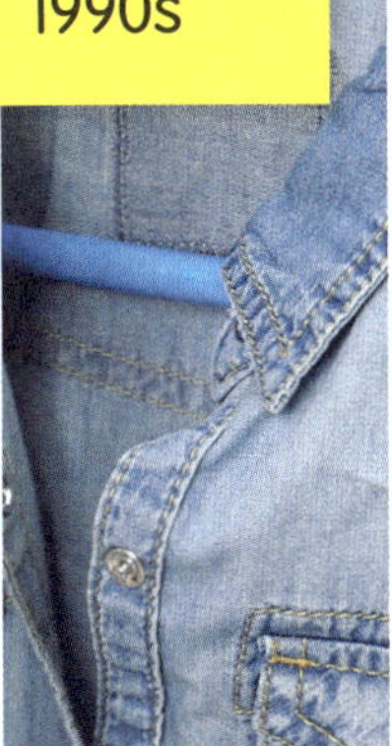

### 1990s

*During the 1990s, people wore shirts, hats, and sunglasses to protect against skin cancer.*

Hats were not popular in the 1970s and 1980s. In the 1990s, people became more aware of skin cancer. Hats became common again.

Many swimming costumes, especially for young children, once again covered much of the body. This was to protect them from the sun.

Box the description of **swimming costumes**

3 Draw people dressed for the beach in the 1970s and 1990s.

| 1970s | 1990s |
| --- | --- |
| | |

GRAMMAR LESSON 8

# Subject-verb Agreement

The **subject** in a sentence is the person or thing that does the action. The **verb** is the action. For example: **The boy** (subject) **runs** (verb) **fast**.

The subject and the verb must agree with each other. For example: **The little girl catches the ball. The girls and boys catch the ball.**

## Read the extract.

In this sentence, **highlight** the **subject** and **circle** the **verb**.

In this sentence, **colour** the **subject** and put a **box** around the **verb**.

In this sentence, **underline** the **subject** and **circle** the **verb**.

In this sentence, **highlight** the **subject** and put a **box** around the **verb**.

### Surviving in the Desert

Water is hard to find in the desert. Desert animals and plants have adapted to survive in dry climates.

Birds and large mammals travel long distances to find water. Other animals get water from the food they eat. The bilby gets water from insects, fruit, seeds and leaves.

Desert plants store water in their trunks, stems and leaves.

A cactus stores water in its stems. It has spines, not leaves. Spines lose less water than leaves.

The Australian saltbush has small leaves that store water. The leaves are waxy, which stops the plant losing water.

**In each sentence, find the subject.**

1. Spines lose less water than leaves.
   - a leaves
   - b water
   - c Spines
   - d less

2. The Australian saltbush has small leaves that store water.
   - a The
   - b The Australian
   - c The Australian saltbush
   - d water

**In each sentence, find the verb.**

3. Warthogs survive without water for several months.
   - a Warthogs
   - b survive
   - c without
   - d months

4. Zebras dig for water in dry riverbeds.
   - a dig
   - b for
   - c water
   - d dry



ACELA1464 Understand how texts are made cohesive through language features

## 5 Complete each sentence with the correct verb.

a Deserts __________ dry places. **is** **are**

b A desert __________ a dry place. **is** **are**

c Desert animals __________ cool underground. **stay** **stays**

d A desert tortoise __________ cool underground. **stay** **stays**

e Hot deserts __________ lots of sand or rock. **has** **have**

f A hot desert __________ lots of sand or rock. **has** **have**

## 6 Colour the verbs that correctly complete each sentence.

**Verbs:** carry, carries, blows, blow, moves, move

a Wind storms __________ sand over great distances.

**Verbs:** digs, live, burrows, burrow, dig, lives

b The marsupial mole __________ underground.

## 7 Fill in the verb.

Deserts __________ very little rainfall.

## ASSESSMENT 4:

# How Can We Attract Birds into Our Gardens?

According to Professor Scott, one way we shouldn't be attracting birds into our gardens is by feeding them. The large number of birds around a bird feeder attracts cats. Also, larger birds, such as parrots, start to take over the area while some, like currawongs, attack the smaller birds and eat their eggs and chicks.

Another reason for not feeding birds is that sometimes they become so used to getting food from us that they stop looking for food in the wild. In addition, the food we give them is often not the right kind and can make them ill.

Professor Scott says the best way to attract birds into our gardens is to create a wild area with native plants in it. The birds will come into the garden to feed on the pollen, seeds and fruit of these plants. They will also eat the insects in the area. In this way, they will eat their natural foods.

We should also make sure there is fresh water for the birds, and we should definitely avoid using chemicals on the plants.

## Circle the correct answer.

**1** Why do people keep bird feeders in their gardens? LITERAL

- **a** to attract cats
- **b** to attract birds
- **c** to make sure birds don't starve
- **d** as ornaments

**2** Why would cats be attracted to birds around a bird feeder? Cats … INFERENTIAL

- **a** prey on birds.
- **b** play with birds.
- **c** like to watch birds.
- **d** steal the birds' food.

3 Which of the following is a big bird? INFERENTIAL

a a lorikeet
b a rosella
c a finch
d a currawong

4 Who is Professor Scott? Professor Scott is most likely a … INFERENTIAL

a scientist.
b farmer.
c reporter.
d photographer.

5 Which is a reason for not feeding birds? If we feed birds, they could … LITERAL

a get fat.
b frighten our pets.
c stop coming into our gardens.
d get sick.

6 What part of a native tree do birds not eat? INFERENTIAL

a leaves
b pollen
c seeds
d fruit

7 Which word is the opposite of *native* in the phrase *native* plants? VOCABULARY

a local
b alien
c natural
d wild

8 Why does Professor Scott say we shouldn't use chemicals on plants? The chemicals might … INFERENTIAL

a kill the plants.
b improve the soil.
c get washed away by rain.
d poison the birds.

9 What is the purpose of the text? CRITICAL

a to retell an event
b to give advice
c to tell a story
d to explain how something works

10 Who is the target audience for this text? People who … CRITICAL

a live in the city.
b have big gardens.
c want more birds in their gardens.
d have cats.

# ANSWERS • PAGES 2–11

## Lesson 21

**Pg 2**

Teacher check passage

**1** b **2** a **3** a **4** b **5** a

**Pg 3**

**A Gecko on the Teacher!**

The gecko jumps onto Mr Mooney's hand. It runs up his arm. It leaps onto his head and waves at us.

Mr Mooney's eyes roll up and his mouth is the shape of an O.

His arms freeze halfway to his head, as if he's too afraid to move.

**6** running up Mr Mooney's arm to his head
**7** scared, afraid
**8** Teacher check

## Lesson 22

**Pg 4**

**A Good Idea**

"Haven't you ever seen a money tree?" asked Mandy.

Tim shook his head. "How do people get a money tree?"

"Easy!" Mandy laughed. "They plant a coin in a pot full of dirt. Then they water it."

"When the coin grows into a tree, flowers grow on it. The flowers turn into money," she told him.

**1** a **2** b **3** c

**Pg 5**

**Trouble!**

Mum didn't like Mandy playing tricks on Tim.

"There's only one thing to do," Mum said. "Take the coins out of your piggybank and stick them on Tim's tree."

"But I was saving up to buy a book!" Mandy told her.

**4** Mandy
**5** to take the coins out of her piggybank and give them to Tim
**6** she played a trick on Tim
**7** a book

## Lesson 23

**Pg 6**

**Happy Birds**

Lots of cages hung in the trees. Grandpa hung Yan's cage with the others.

There were lots of grandpas and lots of songbirds. All the birds whistled.

The air was full of whistles. Grandpa sat on a bench and whistled too.

Yan liked to sing with the other birds. Grandpa liked to whistle with the other grandpas.

**1** d **2** c **3** a

**Pg 7**

Dear Grandpa,

The birds in Australia have bright feathers. Some are grey and pink. Others are white and wear yellow hats. They all sing very loudly.

I wish you could hear the birds, Grandpa. They are happy birds.

I am sure Yan would be happy in Australia. You would be happy too.

I miss going to the park with you, Grandpa.

Love, Ling

**4** Ling says they are bright, colourful and happy
**5** yes: Ling says Australian birds are happy, Grandpa and Yan would be happy, and that she misses going to the park with him

## Lesson 24

**Pg 8**

**More Unusual Pets**

A goose flew in through the window. She landed with a thump. She grumbled as she got up off the floor.

Then a hyena came to the door. He had the hiccups. He saw the goose and laughed.

They began to argue. It went on and on until Stella yelled, "Stop!"

The room was silent. The crocodile stood very still.

**1** b **2** c

**Pg 9**

**Rabbit Chase**

"Help! Help!" yelled the rabbit. "The lion is trying to eat me!"

"I am not," said the lion. He sounded hurt. "I was trying to whisper in your ear. But one of your whiskers tickled my nose. I just slipped.

"Then your foot was in my mouth. I don't know how that happened. Mmmmmm, yummy."

**3** lion/rabbit
**4 a** "Help! Help! The lion is trying to eat me!"
**b** "Mmmmmm, yummy."

## Lesson 25

**Pg 10**

A thirsty ant came to the edge of a river to get a drink. The fast-moving water splashed the ant and knocked it into the river. The ant was in trouble! It tried to swim but it was drowning.

A dove sitting in a tree picked a leaf and dropped it in the river, near the ant. The ant climbed onto the leaf and floated to safety on the bank of the river.

**1** a **2** c, d **3** b

**Pg 11**

A little while later, a hunter came to the edge of the river. He saw the dove sitting in the tree and quickly drew his bow and aimed at the resting bird. The ant saw what was about to happen. It ran over to the hunter and bit his toe as hard as it could. The hunter cried out and dropped his bow. The dove was startled and flew away to safety.

**4** ant/dove
**5 a** bit the hunter's toe as hard as he could
**b** cried out and startled the dove so it could fly away

## Grammar Lesson 1

**Pg 12**

**By the Nose**

Sophie and Alice helped Harry back across the road.

Harry sneezed loudly.

"I smell cats — lots and lots of cats! And I smell Mrs Barker's dog. Woof. Woof smells like he has just had a bath."

"Yes, he has," said Mrs Barker. "And he didn't like it one bit."

Harry kept following his nose down Larkin Street. He named lots of flowers and trees, just by their smell. Sophie and Alice were amazed.

When Harry got to the end of the street, he took a big sniff.

"We are outside your house, Sophie," said Harry. "I can smell your rabbit, Big Ears."

**1** c **2** d **3** a **4** c **5** a

**Pg 13**

**6** bus/thing, baby/person, monkey/animal, museum/place

**7** moon/star

**8** Colour: Amazon, Victoria, April, William, Snowball, Ford
Circle: river, girl, month, boy, cat, car

**9** **a** Street **b** biscuits **c** cat **d** Alice **e** tray/oven

## Lesson 26

**Pg 14**

**Plants in Summer**

*Plants grow quickly in summer.*

Many plants flower in summer. Flowers make seeds. Some flowers, like apple blossoms, become fruit. Fruit grows and ripens in the summer.

In summer, trees are covered in green leaves. The leaves make food for the tree. The trunk grows thicker.

**1** a **2** b **3** c

**Pg 15**

**Summer Food**

*We eat more fresh food in summer.*

Salads are made from fresh summer vegetables. Families enjoy the outdoors by having picnics and barbecues.

Many fruits, such as berries, melons and peaches, are ripe in the summer. Fruit salad is good for you and tastes good too.

**4** fresh foods

**5** vegetables or fruit

**6** outdoors

**7** berries, melons and peaches

**8** fruit salad

## Lesson 27

**Pg 16**

**Finding Water**

*Water is hard to find in a dry habitat.*

Birds and large mammals, such as antelopes, elephants and zebras, travel long distances to find water.

Other animals get water from the food they eat. Bilbies and kangaroo rats get water from insects, fruit, seeds and leaves.

**1** ✔ a, b, e, f ✘ c, d

**Pg 17**

**Conserving Water**

*Desert animals have special water-saving strategies.*

Some animals in dry habitats do not sweat to cool down. This helps the kangaroo rat and the fennec fox to conserve water.

Reptiles have thick skins. Spiders and insects have exoskeletons. These hard, outer shells reduce water loss.

**2** ✔ a, b, d, f ✘ c, e

## Lesson 28

**Pg 18**

**Old Trains**

*The first trains were pulled along by steam engines.*

Steam engines burn coal. The burning coal heats water to make steam. The steam makes the wheels turn.

In the 1800s steam trains were a quick and cheap way to travel for fun as well as for work. Today most steam trains are for tourists.

**1** c **2** c, d

**Pg 19**

**New Trains**

*Today, most trains have diesel or electric engines.*

The new engines are quieter and cleaner than coal-powered steam engines. Diesel trains are often used in country areas. Many electric trains run in cities.

Some electric trains can travel very fast. They are called high-speed trains. The bullet trains in Japan can travel three times faster than a car.

**3** new trains

**4** are diesel or electric.

**5** are quieter and cleaner than coal-powered engines.

## Lesson 29

**Pg 20**

**1** 5, 4, 1, 3, 2 **2** *Answers will vary. Suggested answer:* A drawing of seeds in the field with sunshine and/or rain.

**Pg 21**

**Refining**

*Trucks carry wheat to flour mills. The wheat grains are made into flour.*

People inspect the wheat to make sure it is good quality.

The grain is cleaned and soaked in water for 10 to 20 hours. This separates the outer layer of bran from the soft, inner part. Rollers crush the wheat into a powder called flour.

**3** it is cleaned

**4** rollers crush the wheat into a powder called flour

**5** how to refine wheat

## Lesson 30

**Pg 22**

**1** d **2** 4, 2, 3, 1

**Pg 23**

**3** Then/Next, Next/Then, Finally/At the end

**4** Teacher check

## Grammar Lesson 2

**Pg 24**

**People in Spring**

People spend more time outside in spring.

Spring is an exciting time outdoors. There are many new plants and animals. The air smells fresh. The cold winter is over.

The early sunrise makes waking up easier. The longer days and warm sunshine give many people more energy.

Dandelions make seeds in spring. Children like to blow the seeds away.

Windy days are good for flying kites. Early mornings are good for fishing.

People enjoy eating fresh, spring fruits and vegetables after the cold winter. Strawberries are sweet and juicy in spring.

**1** b **2** c **3** a **4** a

**Pg 25**

**5** circle: big, green, shady, leafy, tall, beautiful

**6** **a** four **b** warmer **c** hottest **d** short **e** cloudy

**7** How many?: twelve, twenty, seven
What colour?: blue, brown, purple
What taste?: bitter, sweet, spicy

**8** colourful/bright, icy/freezing, hungry/starving, delicious/tasty

## Assessment 1

**Pg 26–27**

**1** c **2** b **3** d **4** c **5** a **6** b **7** d **8** a **9** b **10** c

# ANSWERS • PAGES 28–39

## Lesson 31

**Pg 28**

**Thump! Thump! Thump!**

What is that?
"Thump!"
It's coming from the closet. Tim creeps over and slides the door open. A tiny purple alien steps out and pokes Tim on the foot.
"Take me to your weader!"
Tim jumps back on the bed. The alien is only as big as a teddy bear but he has a zap gun. The gun is pointed at Tim.
"Wha ... what?" Tim asks.

**1** a **2** d **3** a

**Pg 29**

**Slime Jelly**

"Here is some slime instead," Tim yells.

Gweep looks in the bowl. "This bad."

Tim looks at the yummy, wobbly, green jelly. "It's really very nice."

Tears form in Gweep's three round eyes. "It's saying no!"

"The slime isn't saying no. It's shaking because it's scared of you."

"Is it scared?" Gweep smiles.

"Of me?"

**4** because it is wobbly and green, just like slime
**5** yes: Gweep smiles because he thinks the jelly is scared of him

## Lesson 32

**Pg 30**

**Beds Are Not Trampolines**

Tim did a star jump. Then he fell off the bed and landed on his nose. He started to cry.

He cried louder and louder.

Mum came running into the room and picked him up.

"Now what have you done?" she asked, looking at his red nose.

"Mandy made me do it," Tim sobbed.

**1** d **2** b **3** b **4** d

**Pg 31**

**Big Trouble**

Tim was in big trouble. He had climbed out our bedroom window to make a water balloon.

As he turned the water on, his balloon flew off. Water sprayed all over the yard.

Just then, Mum and Aunt Beth stepped into the garden. Both of them were sprayed with water. Boy, were they angry!

*Answers will vary. Suggested answers:*
**5** surprised
**6** Climbs out the window. Turns on the tap. Balloon sprays water.
**7** Drawing with Tim looking surprised, Mum looking angry and Aunt Beth shocked.

## Lesson 33

**Pg 32**

**Gee-Gee?**

When I picked him up, Greedy Guts chewed on my fingers. Then he gnawed the strap of my watch.

I put him on the floor and he untied my shoelaces. Then he tried to pull my left sock off. He loved me so much, he wanted to eat me. How could I resist him?

"Mum, please," I begged. "He's perfect."

**1** c **2** c, d

**Pg 33**

Yesterday was Mum's birthday. Aunt Minnie sent Mum a pink, fluffy jacket. Mum hates pink, and she hates fluffy.

"I must ring her to say thank you," Mum said. "Aunt Minnie is a dear to remember my birthday, even if she doesn't remember what I like," Mum said.

"Aunt Minnie is family, and you can't choose your family. Mmmm ... perhaps I could wash it and say that it shrank."

**3** Mum/her birthday
**4 a** hates pink and she hates fluffy.
**b** "Perhaps I could wash it and say that it shrank."

## Lesson 34

**Pg 34**

**1** d
**2** all of the things a person owns in the world

**Pg 35**

**The Courtship of the Yonghy-Bonghy-Bo**

On the coast of Coromandel
Where the early pumpkins blow,
In the middle of the woods
Lived the Yonghy-Bonghy-Bo.
Two chairs, and half a candle,
One old jug without a handle —
These were all his wordly goods:
In the middle of the woods,
These were all the worldly goods
Of the Yonghy-Bonghy-Bo,
Of the Yonghy-Bonghy-Bo.

**3** Teacher check

## Lesson 35

**Pg 36**

A dog had a fresh, meaty bone, which a butcher had thrown to him. He was heading home with his wonderful bone, as fast as he could go.

**1** a **2** b **3** b, d **4** d

**Pg 37**

As the dog crossed a bridge over a pond, he looked down and saw himself reflected in the quiet water. The image was like looking in a mirror.

But the dog thought he saw a real dog carrying another bone — a bone much bigger than his! Without thinking, the dog dropped his bone and leaped at the dog in the pond.

**5** c
**6** quiet, like looking in a mirror
**7** d
**8** *Answers will vary. Suggested answers:* mirrors, windows, shiny surfaces
**9** the same

## Grammar Lesson 3

**Pg 38**

**Bubble Buster**

Buster loved pool parties. He could jump and bomb. He could splash and muck about.

He jumped on Holly's blow up seal. The seal burst. It hissed as it sped across the pool.

"Wow!" said Buster. But Holly didn't think it was funny. Her seal looked like an old plastic bag.

Buster dived under the water when his father pointed an angry finger at him.

Buster saw Holly playing with her bubble maker. As she made bubble after bubble, he began to chase them. Soon he was popping all the bubbles. He liked hearing them pop.

"I'm the bubble buster!" he shouted.

**1** a **2** b **3** c **4** d

**Pg 39**

**5 a** our **b** mine **c** my **d** us **e** ours
**6 a** him **b** it **c** they **d** their **e** his **f** he
**7 a** Buster he **b** wire it **c** Bubbles they **d** Buster his **e** children their

## Lesson 36

**Pg 40**

**Berries to Jam**

*Berries can be eaten fresh. They can also be cooked with sugar to make jam.*

1. Berries grow on small bushes or plants in fields and hothouses.
2. Some farmers use machines to harvest the ripe berries. Others are picked by hand.
3. The berries are washed, trimmed and cut up or mashed. Then, the berries are cooked with sugar until the mixture is thick.
4. Next, the hot jam is poured into jars and sealed to keep it fresh.

**1** grown on small bushes or plants
**2** cooked with sugar until the mixture is thick
**3** into jars
**4** the numbers next to each step

**Pg 41**

**5** Then/Next, Then/Next, After this, Finally
**6** *Suggested answer:* cows in shed, milking the cows, milk tanker, boiling the milk, milk in bottles, store

## Lesson 37

**Pg 42**

**1** ✔ c, d, f ✘ a, b, e
**2** pens and hammers
**3** hammers, pens and calculators
**4** a calculator **5** a blender

**Pg 43**

**1970s**

*Many new tools and gadgets became popular in the 1970s.*

Prior to the 1970s, most schools used books, blackboards, and paper as educational tools.

By the 1970s, many schools had film projectors, record players and tape recorders to help children learn.

By the late 1970s, people began to buy personal computers for their homes.

**6**

| School Tool | Used before 1970 | Used in the 1970s | Used today |
|---|---|---|---|
| Books | ✔ | ✔ | ✔ |
| Blackboards | ✔ | ✔ | ✘ |
| Paper and pencils | ✔ | ✔ | ✔ |
| Film projectors | ✘ | ✔ | ✘ |
| Record players | ✘ | ✔ | ✘ |
| Tape recorders | ✘ | ✔ | ✘ |

**7** books, blackboards, paper and pencils
**8** books, paper and pencils

## Lesson 38

**Pg 44**

**Transport**

*Vehicles, such as cars, buses, trains, planes and boats, transport us from one place to another.*

Some people use transport to make short, daily trips to work or school. Others use it for longer journeys, such as a holiday or business trip overseas.

Public transport is designed for moving large groups of people. Buses, trains, trams, ferries and planes are types of public transport. Private transport includes cars, motorcycles and bicycles.

| 1 | Purpose | Examples |
|---|---|---|
| Private transport | moving small numbers of people | cars, motorcycles and bicycles |
| Public transport | moving large groups of people | buses, trains, trams, ferries and planes |

**2** take people from place to place

**Pg 45**

**Cars**

In the early 1900s, people began to buy their own cars. In 1908, Henry Ford began making cars on an assembly line. His factory made cars at a much faster rate. These mass-produced cars were cheaper to buy.

In the 1950s, many more people owned cars. More cars meant more roads. With more cars on the road, people started to think about car safety. The first seat belts strapped across the driver's lap.

**3**

| Early 1900s | 1908 | 1950s |
|---|---|---|
| People began to buy cars | First assembly line made cars | First seatbelts |

**4** a
**5** c

## Lesson 39

**Pg 46**

Dear Mum,

Today we got up really early and went to the zoo. It was huge! The giraffes had lots of room and the lions hid in the bushes. Dad pretended to be a mountain goat. We bought ice creams after lunch. Boo-boo had chocolate and I had vanilla. Dad carried us when we got really tired. See you tomorrow!

Love, T
xx

**1** Teacher check
**2** Teacher check

**Pg 47**

Dear Anna and Janek,

We arrived in Paris yesterday afternoon. Last night we went up to the top of the Eiffel Tower. The city was all lit up and so pretty. Today we went to three art galleries, so I have sore feet! What have you been doing?

Love, Vicky and Sean

**3** a card you write about your holiday
**4** to tell their friends and family about their holidays
**5** where they are, what they've seen, how they feel
**6** *Answers will vary.* Check postcard has a greeting, details of a holiday and a sign-off.

## Lesson 40

**Pg 48**

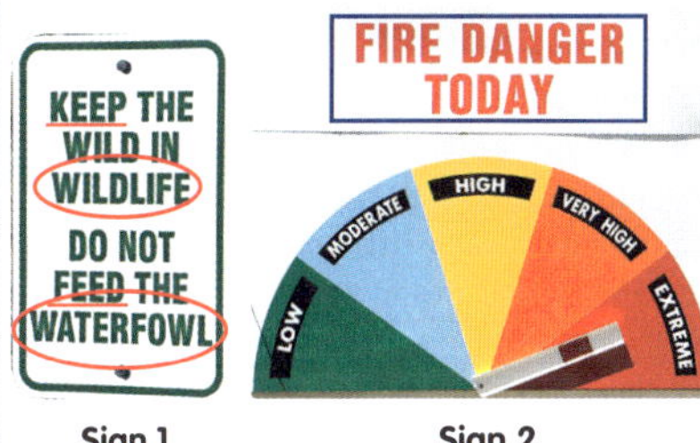


Sign 1 Sign 2

**1 a** that live in the wild
**b** live in the water some of the time
**2** Extreme/Severe/Low

**Pg 49**

**3** easy to break
**4** Handle with care
**5** *Answers will vary. Suggested answers:* glass, crystal, porcelain
**6** *Answers will vary. Suggested answer:* on a package of crystal glasses

## Grammar Lesson 4

**Pg 50**

**The Water Cycle**

Water moves through a continuous cycle.

The sun heats water in oceans, rivers, lakes and creeks. The water turns into water vapour. This is called evaporation.

Water vapour rises and cools. It forms droplets that join together to make clouds. This is called condensation.

When the clouds get heavy, water falls from them as rain, hail or snow. This is called precipitation.

Water can be solid, liquid or gas. Examples are ice (solid), rain (liquid) and steam (gas).

The amount of water on Earth never changes. It's always moving through a part of the water cycle.

**1** c **2** b **3** c **4** b

**Pg 51**

**5 a** rain, hail and snow
**b** trickle, drip, drizzle or pour
**c** wells, tanks, tubs and taps
**d** peaches, pears, grapes and watermelon
**e** watering can, hosepipe, spray bottle and sprinkler

**7 a** Teacher check

**8** Delete comma after
**a** rivers **b** gannets **c** sandcastles
**d** dragonflies **e** sea stars

**9** Teacher check

## Assessment 2

**Pg 52–53**

**1** b **2** c **3** a **4** c **5** b **6** d **7** c **8** a
**9** d **10** b

## Lesson 41

**Pg 54**

**Imagine This, Imagine That**

"It's easy. One person starts imagining something that doesn't exist, say a flying car, and the next person has to add to it," said Luke.

"So you could imagine a flying car shaped like a fish," said Aunt Stella.

Sophie understood. "And the flying car shaped like a fish could spray fireworks from its wheels."

**1** a **2** b **3** d

**Pg 55**

**Art Eyes**

"Look out for colours, patterns, shapes, textures and shadows that catch your attention. Draw them in your journal and collect as much treasure as you can!" Aunt Stella cried.

Sophie liked the shapes and colours of the shells. She collected lots of shells of all shapes, sizes, colours and patterns. Sophie also rubbed some rock textures into her journal and drew a rough sketch of the beach. But her most precious find was a piece of blue, weathered glass.

**4** shells
**5** a sketch of the beach
**6** precious
**7** *Answers will vary. Suggested answer:* One day I found a beautiful peacock's feather. I took it home and put it in a jar. It's the most precious thing I have.

## Lesson 42

**Pg 56**

**Smelly and Stuck**

Jake's toenail went PING! Jake spun around like a corkscrew. And there he stuck.

Everybody pushed and shoved. People with cameras took photos. People with notebooks asked questions.

"What does it feel like to be trapped by your toenail, Jake? they asked.

The sacks were full of fertiliser. The longest toenail in the world was no fun anymore.

**1** b **2** e **3** a

**Pg 57**

**Sam's Cool Idea**

The longest toenail in the world was growing.

Longer and wider and taller! And it was growing FAST!

It curled three times round his body. It shot past his ears. It twisted over his head. It snaked up past the diving board.

Jake gasped as his toenail snaked and grew. As big as himself ... as tall as a tree ... as big as a house ... as tall as a crane.

**4** *Answers will vary. Suggested answer:* a drawing of a boy with a very long toenail.
**5** *Answers will vary. Suggested answer:* I would feel excited to be different to everyone else.
**6** Jake gasped

## Lesson 43

**Pg 58**

**The Home Haircut**

"Easy," said Jan as she cut. "Piece of cake!"

I remember when Jan said cooking was easy. We spent an afternoon scraping burnt food off the stove.

Jan also told me that camping was easy. The tent fell on top of us during the night.

By three o'clock on Saturday afternoon there was more hair on the bathroom floor than on my head.

**1** c **2** c **3** a

**Pg 59**

**The Home Haircut**

"Look in the mirror, Freya," said Jan.

I did. There was a lot of face and not much hair.

"Is it all right?" Jan said, looking worried.

"One side is longer than the other," I said softly.

Jan cut some more. Snip. Snip. Snip.

In the mirror, I looked strange. My hair was gone. Bits stuck out all over the place.

Jan's face was white.

**4** she doesn't like it
**5** she says, "I looked strange."
**6** *Answers will vary. Suggested answer:* Drawing of Freya with short, uneven hair, and Jan looking very nervous.

## Lesson 44

**Pg 60**

**Ringmaster Roy:** Chuckles, perhaps you could teach Snoz about being a clown.
**Narrator:** Chuckles had a great time dressing Snoz and painting him with make-up. But when Snoz saw himself in the mirror, he hid under the table.
**Snoz:** Not funny! Too scary! Snoz is scared!
**Narrator:** Snoz began to cry. Seeing a Snozalot cry made Chuckles cry too.
**Chuckles:** (sobbing) That is the saddest thing I have ever seen. A sobbing Snozalot!

**1** a **2** b, c

**Pg 61**

**Ringmaster Roy:** Tell me troupe, what can Snoz the Snozalot Monster do?
**Chuckles:** I will tell you what he cannot do. He cannot make you laugh.
**Bendy Betty:** He cannot bend.
**Max Manyhands:** He cannot juggle.
**Ringmaster Roy:** I see, I see. I see. And I know he can't fly though the air.
**Chuckles:** He's a nice monster.
**Bendy Betty:** A lovely monster, really.
**Max Manyhands:** But Snoz has no place in Circus Bizurkus.

**3** Snoz the Snozalot Monster/Circus Bizurkus
**4 a** can't do circus acts.
**b** no place in Circus Bizurkus.

## Lesson 45

**Pg 62**

The gnat dived at the lion and stung him on the nose. The lion was furious. He swiped at the gnat, but only ended up scratching himself with his sharp claws. The gnat attacked the lion again and again, and the lion raged.

**1** d **2** a, e **3** d

**Pg 63**

Finally, the lion was worn out. He was dripping with blood from his own scratches and he lay down, defeated by the gnat. The gnat buzzed away to tell the whole Animal Kingdom about his victory over the lion, but instead he flew straight into a spider's web.

**4** b
**5 a** defeated by the gnat
**b** worn out the lion
**6** don't be too quick to claim victory

## Grammar Lesson 5

**Pg 64**

**Magic and Computers**

Ellie knew about magic. She read stories about magic. In stories things happened and no one could explain why.

Gary never thought about magic, but he didn't read much. He was Ellie's brother and two years older.

When Ellie asked Gary if computers were magic, Gary laughed.

"Computers only do what they are programmed to do," said Gary.

"What does programmed mean?" Ellie asked.

Gary tried to explain. "A computer is built by people to work things out. People write programs and the computer follows the program's instructions."

**1** a **2** c **3** d **4** b

**Pg 65**

**5** **a** and **b** or/and **c** and/but **d** or/and **e** but/and

**6** **a** Ellie likes to read and/but Gary likes to play computer games.

**b** You can use my tablet but you must look after it.

**c** Are you going to write the story or are you going to type it?

**7** Teacher check

## Lesson 46

**Pg 66**

**Finding Fossils**

Places where rocks are eroding might have fossils. Creek banks, dry riverbeds and cliff faces are all good places to look. Most fossils are covered by a thick layer of rock. At some sites, explosives blow up the rock and bulldozers cart it away. Often the whole block of rock, with its bones, is cut out. This is taken back to the lab where the bones are carefully removed.

**1** 5, 3, 2, 4, 6, 1

**2** museum

**Pg 67**

**Giant Jigsaw Puzzles**

Putting a dinosaur back together takes skill, patience and a lot of time.

Using photos and drawings, the skeleton is laid out on the floor and then put back together from the ground up.

Most bones are too fragile to become a skeleton in a museum. A plaster or plastic cast is made. It is rare to find a complete skeleton—most museums' dinosaurs are put together with extra parts.

**3** *Answers will vary. Suggested answer:* Drawings of the bones. Skeleton on the floor. Making a cast. Skeleton put together.

## Lesson 47

**Pg 68**

**A World-changing Gizmo**

It all began in 1947. That's when three scientists invented the transistor.

The three scientists were from the Bell Laboratories. Their names were John Bardeen, Walter Brattain and William Shockley.

The first transistor was about the size of your thumb. It was made from a paperclip, gold foil, wire and a bit of plastic. Transistors were first used in telephones.

Transistors are in computers, the Internet, mobile phones, TVs, video cameras, calculators, hand-held games, radar, satellites and night vision technology.

**1** c **2** b **3** b

**Pg 69**

**Why Didn't I Think of That?**

Dr Nakamatsu is a modern inventor. He holds the world record for the most patents and inventions. Dr Nakamatsu has over 3200 inventions.

Dr Nakamatsu often came up with ideas underwater. He invented a notepad that he could use underwater to write down his ideas.

Dr Nakamatsu only sleeps four hours a night. He says the best time for new ideas is between midnight and 4 am. He has two special rooms that help him think.

**4** He had ideas underwater but couldn't write them down.

**5** He invented a notepad that he could use underwater.

**6** Teacher check

## Lesson 48

**Pg 70**

**1**

| | Travels on and between | | | | | Travel for | | | Time on board | | On board | | |
|---|---|---|---|---|---|---|---|---|---|---|---|---|---|
| | rivers | harbours | lakes | cities | countries | work | holiday | school | Minutesor hours | Days orweeks | shops | movie theatres | restrooms |
| ferry | ✔ | ✔ | ✔ | ✔ | ✔ | ✔ | ✔ | ✔ | ✔ | | | | ✔ |
| cruise ship | | | | ✔ | ✔ | | ✔ | | | ✔ | ✔ | ✔ | ✔ |

**2** restrooms

**3** cities and countries

**Pg 71**

**4**

| Boat | What does it do? | How many people can it hold? | Interesting fact |
|---|---|---|---|
| destroyer | protect bigger, slower ships | 300 | moves fast |
| submarine | travel quickly underwater | 150 | moves fast |
| aircraft carriers | carry planes | 5000 | biggest ship in the navy |

**5** They are all navy vessels.

## Lesson 49

**Pg 72**

To: Kosoko

From: Matilda

Please come to my: 8th birthday party

Where: Memorial Park, Dale Street

When: Saturday, 14 September

RSVP: 0499 853 627

**1** a

**2** d

**3** b

**4** Teacher check

**Pg 73**

Dear Amy,

I am going to have a sleepover at my house next Friday. Do you want to come? We will play games, eat lots of pizza and stay up really late. Mum says that she can drive you home the next morning. My address is 48 Trig Street. Please let me know if your mum and dad say it is OK to come. It will be lots of fun!

Bye,

Hua

**5** Teacher check

## Lesson 50

**Pg 74**

**Hoofed Mammals**

*Hoofed mammals eat plants. They are herbivores. Zebras, giraffes and elephants are all hoofed mammals.*

Many hoofed mammals live in groups called herds. They often live on open plains or grasslands. The herd moves from place to place in search of food. Zebras and wildebeests live in large herds.

Elephants are the largest land animals. They live in family groups called herds. Baby elephants feed on mother's milk for two years while they grow.

**1** d **2** c

# ANSWERS • PAGES 75–88

**Pg 75**

**Monkeys and Apes**

*Monkeys and apes are mammals called primates. They are warm-blooded, furry animals that suckle their young.*

Baboons, mandrills and howlers are all monkeys. Monkeys are very good climbers. They use their hands, feet and tails to help them climb.

Apes are larger than monkeys. Chimpanzees, gibbons, orangutans and gorillas are all apes. Apes do not have tails.

Gorillas are the largest of all the apes and are tailless. They live in family groups.

**3**

| small | larger | largest |
|---|---|---|
| Monkeys (baboons, mandrills and howlers) | Apes (chimpanzees, gibbons, orangutans) | Gorillas |

**4** Monkeys have tails but apes don't.
**5** "Apes do not have tails."

## Grammar Lesson 6

**Pg 76**

**Beatrix Potter**

Beatrix Potter is famous for writing children's books. Her best-known book is *The Tale of Peter Rabbit*.

Beatrix was born in England in 1866. Six years later, her brother Bertram was born.

As children, Beatrix and Bertram enjoyed sketching. Beatrix spent hours copying art from books and artworks.

In her twenties, Beatrix became very interested in studying fungi. She even wrote a paper on them. But scientists did not value her work because she was a woman.

After that, Beatrix began to focus on her art. She also started writing stories. In 1901 she published *The Tale of Peter Rabbit* herself for her family and friends. A year later, a company agreed to publish it. It was a huge success.

**1** b **2** a **3** c

**Pg 77**

**4 a** before **b** Next **c** after
**d** tonight **e** finally
**5** Teacher check
**6 B** Eventually/Later **C** After
**D** Eventually/Later **E** Today

## Assessment 3

**Pg 78–79**

**1** d **2** b **3** b **4** b **5** c **6** c **7** a **8** b
**9** c **10** b

## Lesson 51

**Pg 80**

**Zac the Champion**

Mr McFee asked Zac to read aloud. Zac said he couldn't find his glasses. He said his mother would look for them after work.

"Can't you see without your glasses?" I asked.

Zac shook his head.

After school, Zac came to my place. We played computer games on my Dad's computer.

Zac could see well enough to play them. He won every game.

**1** c **2** a **3** b

**Pg 81**

**Zac Skips School**

The next day Zac didn't come to school. Nina and Danny went to Zac's house after school. He was watching a cartoon.

When he saw them he rolled around on the floor. He held his stomach.

"I have a very bad migraine," he said. "Mum's going to take me to the doctor."

**4** unwell
**5** Zac held his stomach and said he had a migraine.
**6** When you have a migraine your head is sore not your stomach.
**7** He doesn't want to go to school.

## Lesson 52

**Pg 82**

**The Sniffles**

Vinnie raced in the front door. His bag skidded across the living room floor.

"What's going on in here?" Vinnie's mum stood in the doorway, hands on her hips.

Vinnie walked over and picked up his bag.

"Sorry, Mum. I'm in a bit of a hurry."

"What about a snack?"

"I'm not hungry."

Mary stood in shock as she watched him run up the stairs.

**1** a **2** b, c **3** c

**Pg 83**

**Dr Hacker**

Vinnie pulled the ad from his pocket and dialled the number.

"Hello," said the voice on the other end of the line.

"Are you Dr. Hacker?" asked Vinnie.

"That's right."

Vinnie explained his problem.

"Never fear, young Vinnie. I'll be there in a flash," said Dr. Hacker.

Vinnie hung up. Smoke filled the hall and a flash of light blinded him.

Dr. Hacker waved away the smoke.

"Show me your sick computer."

**4** It's a computer problem.
**5** He is magical.
**6** The text says, "Smoke filled the hall and a flash of light blinded him."

## Lesson 53

**Pg 84**

**1** Teacher check **2** Teacher check

**Pg 85**

**3** Teacher check
**4** Teacher check
**5** Teacher check

## Lesson 54

**Pg 86**

A man, just one –
also a fly, just one –
in the huge drawing room

**Kobayashi Issa**

**1** a, d **2** b, d **3** b **4** b

**Pg 87**

Warm snug speckled egg
Dappled light fading quickly
Soft crack of split shell

**Alysha Hodge**

**5** d **6** d **7** c **8** d

## Lesson 55

**Pg 88**

A hungry fox was looking for food. She saw bunches of juicy, plump grapes growing high up on a farmer's fence.

"I will have those grapes. I'm starving!" she said.

**1** d **2** b, d **3** b

Pg 89

The fox ran at the fence and leaped as high as she could. It was a great leap—but it wasn't high enough. She hadn't even reached the lowest bunch of grapes.

The fox tried again. She ran and leaped and it was another wonderful leap. But once again, she did not jump high enough to reach the fruit. She didn't give up though.

**4** b

**5 a** a great leap but it wasn't high enough

**b** again and it was a wonderful leap but it wasn't high enough

## Grammar Lesson 7

Pg 90

Has Anyone Seen My Chook?

Hazel followed the seawall past the flooded houses until she reached the coconut grove. Nearby, perched on the branch of a dead mango tree, was Loki, the chicken boy. Beside him sat his six fat hens.

"Have you seen my chook, Violet?" Hazel asked Loki.

"No, I haven't seen her. Maybe the waves got her. Maybe a big fish got her."

Hazel shook her head. "Violet always flies up high when the tide comes in. Are you taking your hens to school today?"

"No, there are too many. I am taking this." Loki reached into his shirt pocket and pulled out a tiny, chirping chick.

**1** c **2** a **3** b **4** d

Pg 91

**5 a** eats **b** named **c** built **d** walk **e** waded **f** picks

**6** colour: hop, swallow, fly, sleep, peck

**7** Teacher check

## Lesson 56

Pg 92

Bengal Tigers

*Some Bengal tigers live in the mangrove forests of India and Bangladesh.*

Tigers hunt mammals, such as wild boars. Bengal tigers also eat saltwater crabs and fish.

Tigers are quick and powerful hunters. They have soft foot pads that help them quietly stalk prey. Their striped coats help tigers hide in the forest. Every tiger has a different pattern of stripes.

**1** d **2** a, b, d

**3** Drawing of a wild boar, crab and fish

Pg 93

Hippopotamuses

*Hippos live in swampy lakes and rivers in Africa.*

Hippos spend the day in the water. A hippo's eyes, ears and nostrils are on the top of its head. It can watch for danger while the rest of its body is underwater.

Hippos nurse their young and even sleep underwater. Hippos do not truly swim. They run or walk along the river bed.

Hippos are often aggressive. They open their mouths to warn off intruders.

**4** Drawing of a labelled hippopotamus

## Lesson 57

Pg 94

**1**

| Vegetable | Cooler weather | Warmer weather | Quick to grow | Longer to grow |
|---|---|---|---|---|
| carrot | ✔ | | | ✔ |
| corn | | ✔ | | ✔ |
| capsicum | | ✔ | ✔ | |
| onion | ✔ | | | ✔ |
| winter lettuce | ✔ | | ✔ | |
| tomato | | ✔ | | ✔ |

**2** c, d, e

Pg 95

Cows and Sheep

*Some farmers raise large herds of cattle. Others raise large flocks of sheep.*

Farmers raise herds of cows, called cattle, for their meat and hides. Leather is made into shoes, clothes and furniture. Cattle eat grass in fields or are fed hay and grain.

Dairy cows make milk. Milk can be made into cheese, yogurt and ice cream.

Farmers raise sheep for their wool, meat and milk. Farmers shear sheep once a year. The wool can be made into sweaters, blankets and carpets.

**3**

Sheep: wool
Sheep & Cattle: meat, milk
Cattle: leather

## Lesson 58

Pg 96

How a jet engine works

Jet engines burn a mixture of fuel and air. This makes hot gases, which give thrust. Thrust gets a plane off the ground and keeps it moving.

**1** b **2** 3, 4, 1, 5, 2

Pg 97

Swing Wings

Wide wings help get a plane off the ground. They also slow it down in the sky. Swing wings solve this problem. On fighters like the F-14 Tomcat, the wings sweep back once the jet is in the air.

**3** the wide wings

**4** out to the sides

**5** after take-off

**6** they swing out to the sides again

## Lesson 59

Pg 98

Healthy Foods

*Your body needs a variety of good foods to grow and stay healthy.*

The food we eat is called our diet. A balanced diet contains a wide variety of foods.

Carbohydrates in foods such as bread and rice give us energy. Other foods, like fruits and vegetables, are full of vitamins and minerals.

We need protein to make muscles, skin and hair. Meat and eggs are high-protein foods. We need calcium for our teeth and bones. Dairy foods, like cheese and milk, are high in calcium.

**1**

| | Why we need them | Examples |
|---|---|---|
| Carbohydrates | give us energy | Teacher check |
| Fruit and vegetables | full of vitamins and minerals | Teacher check |
| Protein | make muscles, skin and hair | Teacher check |
| Dairy | good for teeth and bones | Teacher check |

Pg 99

Grains

A healthy diet should include grains, such as wheat, rice and corn.

Some grain is cooked and eaten whole. These are wholegrain foods. Other grain is ground into flour to make bread, pasta and cereals. All grains have carbohydrates, which give the body energy.

Some wholegrain foods are corn on the cob, rice and wholegrain bread. They are high in fibre. Wholegrains contain magnesium, a mineral that helps build strong bones and teeth.

**2** carbohydrates which the body can use for energy

**3** fibre and magnesium

**4** building strong bones and teeth

## Lesson 60

**Pg 100**

**1800s**

*During the 1800s, machinery for making clothes was invented. More factories were built. Textiles became mass-produced.*

Before machinery, weavers and tailors made clothes by hand.

Sewing machines were invented and then mass-produced during the 1800s. This allowed women at home to make clothing quickly and easily. Clothes of the 1800s were often uncomfortable to wear. Women wore bone corsets that laced up tightly.

**1** a **2** b, e

**Pg 101**

**1990s**

*During the 1990s, people wore shirts, hats, and sunglasses to protect against skin cancer.*

Hats were not popular in the 1970s and 1980s. In the 1990s, people became more aware of skin cancer. Hats became common again.

Many swimming costumes, especially for young children, once again covered much of the body. This was to protect them from the sun.

**3** *Answers will vary. Suggested answers:* A drawing of people in the 1970s at the beach without a hat and a drawing of people in the 1990s wearing long sleeved bathing suits.

## Grammar Lesson 8

**Pg 102**

**Surviving in the Desert**

Water is hard to find in the desert. Desert animals and plants have adapted to survive in dry climates.

Birds and large mammals travel long distances to find water. Other animals get water from the food they eat. The bilby gets water from insects, fruit, seeds and leaves.

Desert plants store water in their trunks, stems and leaves.

A cactus stores water in its stems. It has spines, not leaves. Spines lose less water than leaves.

The Australian saltbush has small leaves that store water. The leaves are waxy, which stops the plant losing water.

**1** c **2** c **3** b **4** a

**Pg 103**

**5 a** are **b** is **c** stay **d** stays
**e** have **f** has

**6 a** colour: carry, blow, move
**b** colour: digs, burrows, lives

**7** Teacher check

## Assessment 4

**Pg 104–105**

**1** b **2** a **3** d **4** a **5** d **6** a **7** b **8** d **9** b **10** c